Jewel of Britannia

A World War I Romance

by
Marian Keen

Marian Keen

Keen Ideas Publishing | Vancouver, Canada

JEWEL OF BRITANNIA
A World War I Romance

Library and Archives Canada Cataloguing in Publication

Title: Jewel of Britannia : a World War I romance / by Marian Keen.
Names: Keen, Marian, 1935- author.
Description: Includes index.
Identifiers: Canadiana (print) 20210192305 | Canadiana (ebook) 2021019233X | ISBN 9781988220253
   (softcover) | ISBN 9781988220260 (PDF) | ISBN 9781988220277 (HTML)
Classification: LCC PS8621.E355 J49 2021 | DDC C813/.6—dc23

Table of Contents

Dedication

* * * * *

Dedicated to all veterans whose lives were
interrupted, marred, or lost.

It is our duty to honour them by living helpful,
respectful, and happy lives.

* * * * *

Marian Keen

* * * * *

The beautiful thing
about young love
is the truth
in our hearts
that it will last forever.

Atticus

* * * * *

Prologue

1914: The Threat

The two men stepped out of the black Mercedes, pulling their collars against the blowing snow. Still hungover from celebrating the 1914 New Year, they walked towards the administration offices of the Krupp's munitions factory.

"Have you any idea why Herr Krupp sent for two railroad officials, Karl?"

"I was not informed, Erik. Everything at the factory is top secret. Why? Have you guessed?"

"Well, our railroad transports goods. Krupp's company makes munitions. I imagine we will be asked to transport a load of guns. Even my little son can figure that one out!"

"I suppose you're right, Erik. All of Europe wants war. It's in the air! The Kaiser is wisely preparing so that Germany will prevail."

They entered the building. Erik lowered his voice. "We are meeting with Professor Rausenbergen, the director of design. I wonder, did the professor design a gun to play a dirge when it hits a target? Or did he design a gun that can't miss?"

"Nein, Erik. Don't be ridiculous! German soldiers don't miss!"

They were escorted to the factory floor by the professor and Herr Krupp, himself. To their astonishment they were soon standing under the largest howitzer they could ever have imagined.

The challenge presented to them was how to transport this 150 ton howitzer, with its stationary carriage and concrete foundation, along with enough shells to keep the beast armed.

Dwarfed by the menacing two-storey cannon, Karl and Erik walked around it in awe, knees shaking.

Herr Krupp stood, feet apart with his thumbs hooked into his vest. "I call it Dicke Bertha in honour of my wife, Bertha. Beautiful, isn't she?"

Professor Rausenbergen said, "As requested, this howitzer will smash reinforced fortifications, and conquer all for our Kaiser Willhelm."

"It will require many rail cars, maybe six," ventured Erik.

The professor snorted. "At least ten will be needed! Bertha must be dismantled, and of course the supports will take additional cars. You figure it out and let us know when you're ready. And there are two howitzers, one for each train."

Later, in the Mercedes, Erik said to Karl, "Germany cannot lose any conflict with that monster of a weapon."

"I pity the poor soldiers pitting their puny

weapons against Big Bertha. She'll bury them."

"That giant is terrifying. Germany will win any conflict in weeks. We'll take over all of Europe!" added Erik.

"With Big Bertha we'll rule the whole world!"

The two men gloated in triumph as they drove away, saying, "Watch out world, Bertha's going to bury you!"

Marian Keen

1. Innocence

Dorie grasped the pale pink skirt of her dress and crossed her feet as she curtsied the way her mother had taught her. The mirror over her dressing table was too small to see if she had done it correctly, so she stepped back for a full view and banged into her bed. She slipped and caught her balance by reaching for the bedpost.

"Oh dear, these new shoes are slippery!"

She stepped over to her dressing table and smoothing her dress, sat on the low stool and peered into the mirror. She smiled. No pimples. She picked up the lipstick. Her hand trembled even though she'd practiced all week to apply it properly. Bracing her elbow on the table she carefully dabbed the soft pink to her lips. Finally satisfied, she smiled again to check that she hadn't put pink on her teeth.

From downstairs she heard the front door and her mother's voice. She quietly left her room and entered her parents' bedroom. Stepping to her mother's bureau, she put a quick dab of perfume behind each ear, and ducked out again for the stairs.

"I saw you!" whispered pajama-clad Donny peeking out of his bedroom.

"Just looking for Mom," said Dorie.

"She's downstairs," said Donny, "She just let

Florence in."

"Thank you. Now get back in bed," said Dorie as she stepped down to the front hall as casually as she could in her slippery shoes. Flo looked up at Dorie and said, "No one can wear pink as well as you can!"

"Thanks Flo. That green dress is perfect with your red hair," said Dorie. "Shall we go?"

"Wait!" said Dorie's Mom. "This is your first formal dance, Dorothy; I want to hug my grown-up daughter!"

Dorie's father came into the hallway. "Beautiful! Beautiful! I can't believe how fast you girls have grown into young women. Kiss for your Dad, Dorie?"

Dorie kissed her Dad's cheek.

"You smell good!" he said.

"Doesn't she!" said her Mom dryly, recognizing her own best perfume.

"Let's go!" said Dorie, urging Flo to leave to avoid a reprimand on the stolen fragrance. And the girls eagerly left for the Community Hall full of anticipation.

It was the late spring of 1914 in Britannia Beach, the copper mining town on BC's west coast. The evening was balmy. This was the high school graduation dance that included the third year students, and excitement filled the air. Dorie would never forget it.

Music bounced through the air and enticed the girls up the stairs and into the hall. But the dance floor was empty, even though the musicians played a catchy beat. Chairs lined the hall on both sides, with girls seated primly on the left and boys slouching casually on the right. No one was dancing.

A bit let down, Dorie and Flo found seats together and attempted to look poised and cheerful. After fifteen minutes, disappointment clouded Dorie's face. Flo glanced at her and said, "Don't worry. It always starts like this."

Flo was a year older than Dorie and had been to the dance the year before. "The boys are always shy at first." she added.

The music paused. Chaperones—Mr. Weeks, the math teacher, and Miss Tillman, the English teacher—sat just to the left of the stage. Mr. Weeks rose and announced, "We will now have the Schottische! You all know this dance; you learned it at school. Now take your places on the dance floor."

Dorie paired up with Arthur. He was short but he knew the dance. Dorie was grateful that he hopped on time. Dorie saw Flo across the circle. Flo was dancing with Jerry who was tall, awkward and flat-footed.

Poor Flo! thought Dorie, and this is such a long dance!

Unnoticed by the dancers, a half-dozen young men from the miners' dorm in Camp Jane slipped in the front door. Standing there they watched the Schottische parade. As Dorie twirled she felt their eyes and blushed wondering how she looked dancing with Arthur who was so short!

Finally the Schottische finished. The boys escorted the girls to their seats as the band began a waltz. Arthur asked Dorie for the waltz.

"Maybe the next one," Dorie said, "I'm out of breath." She looked down to avoid his eyes and another pair of shoes appeared as Arthur's disappeared. She looked up and above broad shoulders to deep blue smiling eyes and felt a surge of hope swell in her chest.

"May I?" the young man asked extending his hand.

Dorie rose taking his hand and dropped a quick curtsy before she was swept onto the dance floor. Waltzing lightly and smoothly, it felt heavenly. He waltzes so much better than Dad, thought Dorie.

The waltz ended far too soon. But grasping her hand firmly, the young man walked her in the intervening parade around the room as was the custom.

"My name is Robert Roman Chase. Thank you for the waltz; are you willing to dance another?"

"Oh, yes, Robert!" said Dorie. "My name is Dorothy Juliet Sanders."

"My friends call me Rob."

"My friends call me Dorie."

They smiled at each other as the piano, bass, and violins began a foxtrot. Robert twirled Dorie around and they moved smoothly and briskly around the floor to the music.

At the next break, Robert still held her hand as they walked around the floor.

"Did you say your middle name is Juliet?" asked Rob.

Dorie blushed, "My mother thought it a romantic name."

"Tis," said Robert, "but I think Jules is more fitting…"

"Jewels?" asked Dorie.

"… as in opal; you look like an opal gem in that dress!"

"You said your middle name is Romeo?" asked Dorie.

"Close!" Rob chuckled. "It's Roman. A family name. But you can call me Romeo if you like! Just don't call me Bob."

Dorie laughed, "Romeo and Juliet! How perfect!"

The music began again. They danced all night. Dorie didn't think about her friend Flo until it was time to go home. Flo was nowhere to be seen!

"I'll walk you home," said Rob.

"Thank you!" said Dorie gratefully.

And on the way home, Dorie experienced her first kiss.

Dorie couldn't wait to tell Flo about Rob. The two girls met on the school steps the next day, just minutes before class.

"I'm in love!" gushed Flo. "Charlie is a sweetheart! I love his sandy hair and big brown eyes. He dances well and he's such a sweet-talker! I hope you had a good time. Oh dear! Gotta go! I'm late for my exam!"

Dorie couldn't get in a word.

The last weeks of school flew. Graduation arrived on the last day of June. Flo wore an ivory dress made from the lace of her mother's wedding dress. The Hall was jammed with parents and friends. Dorie ushered guests and gave out programs. The crowd of parents and teachers spoke in hushed tones about an assassination in Europe. Dorie overheard that the Austrian Archduke, Franz Ferdinand, and his wife had been shot in Europe. She hoped such a horrible murder so far away wouldn't mar Flo's graduation. But the ceremony went smoothly and congratulations enveloped the graduates.

Flo's eyes sparkled as she showed Dorie her engagement ring. Charlie was there with Flo's parents and they looked proud and happy.

As summer began, Dorie worked for her father in his dry goods store relieving her mother so she could garden, preserve jams, and can tomatoes and beans for the winter.

Dorie spent as much time as she could with Robert who lived in the miners' dorm in Camp Jane, high up the mountain. Rob volunteered to bring supplies up the mountain from the docks whenever the Britannia steamship called. Dorie volunteered to collect goods for her father's business, so they saw each other regularly on the docks.

Sitting on the dock one day, waiting for the steamship, Dorie asked Rob, 'Have you ever seen any gold when you work the rock?"

"There's a glint now and then but it's mostly copper sulfite and lead, and silver's just a dull grey dirt. It's hard work and boring. I don't want to mine for the rest of my life."

"What do you want to do?" asked Dorie.

"Go back to school for my teaching certificate and

spend my life with you, Jules," Rob said, playfully nudging her with his shoulder.

"You're very sweet, Rob," said Dorie.

"You're a jewel to me, girl!"

Then Dorie's father's gruff voice announced, "Up and at 'em, Romeo! Here's the steamship!"

July was hot and filled with picnics, swimming and baseball games.

Dorie's mom asked for her help one morning. "Donny is too clumsy. He'll get strawberry jam all over himself and break a jar or two, I'm sure."

Dorie washed and scrubbed away at dusty jars, setting them carefully on the drainboard. Her mom tended the simmering strawberry pot and dried the jars and lids.

"Dorothy, I want a word with you about Robert."

"Yes, Mom?"

"I understand his family lives in Alberta. I can see that he's a nice young man, very polite and hardworking, but ..."

"But?"

"Is he wanting to be a miner?"

"No, he wants to be a teacher. He's mining to pay for his further education."

"Mmm, I see. That will take some time."

Her mother touched her on the shoulder. Dorie

turned to her. Her mom said seriously, "Dorie, keep your level head, dear girl. Don't get carried away and get into trouble." Dorie knew exactly what her mother was saying.

"I won't. I promise."

"Good girl. Now help me fill the jars."

Later that afternoon, Dorie and Rob took her brother swimming at the beach. Her mother took Dorie's place in the store.

Donny stumbled on a rock and fell into water over his head. He bobbed up gasping. Rob moved fast. He took Donny's hands as if they were playing a game while moving to a more shallow area along the shore. He let Donny go when he touched bottom and jumped up, smiling.

Rob returned to Dorie who said, "Nice going, Romeo, Donny didn't have a chance to panic."

"Donny's a nice kid; he's almost swimming and luckily he's not afraid of the water. It's important not to panic in tight situations."

Dorie looked at Rob thoughtfully; then said quietly, "I love you, Romeo!"

Robert grinned at her, "That's a relief, Jules! I've loved you from the very first time I saw you dancing with Shorty!"

The end of July heralded the Midsummer's Picnic. The Britannia Beach community invited the families from Mount Sheer, located high above Britannia Beach, and the miners from Camp Jane. Competitions, sports, games, and dancing encouraged everyone to take part. The mine and the mill were closed for the day.

Dorie had entered the baking contest with her lemon chiffon pie. While the judging was underway, Dorie's father asked for a word with Robert, who was grilling hot dogs.

"Yes, sir. Can I help you?"

"Yes, Robert. I'd like to talk to you about Dorie."

"About your daughter, sir?" said Robert, looking up from the grill.

"Dorie is only seventeen, and has one more year of school. I'd like her to finish high school before she takes on more responsibilities. You understand. To put it bluntly, I do not wish to give her my blessing to marriage until she is nineteen. I hope that sits well with your intentions?"

"Perfectly, sir, perfectly. How would you like your dog, sir?"

"With all the trimmings, Rob. Thank you. I'm glad we had this little talk."

Less than a week later the devastating news hit Britannia Beach.

"Invasion of Belgium!" ran the headline. People

scrambled to get their hands on the newspapers coming from the steamship.

Dorie's father was one of the first to read that war had begun in Europe. It was clear that as part of the Commonwealth, Canada was now at war with Germany and Austria-Hungary. His eyes scanned the details of the invasion. The poor Belgians didn't stand a chance as their old fortifications crumbled under explosive attacks from gigantic cannons. People fled as buildings were leveled, only to be shot as they ran.

Surviving witnesses described the monstrous weapons used in the attack. 'It was enormous, over 20 feet high, with a huge gaping mouth!' said one. 'It took dozens and dozens of men to arm it, and fire it. But once it was fired it hit a building from a far distance, exploding and leveling the building,' said another. 'Some people ran, others hid. I only escaped by luck,' reported a third.

Other survivors had also witnessed the Big Bertha howitzer in action, including two children who had hid during the first moments of invasion. Brother and sister, Matilda and Maximilian huddled under hay in the back of a chicken coop, behind the remains of the big house they had called home. Sounds of the gunshots that had killed her mother and father still echoed in Matilda's head as she held her sleeping brother and watched anxiously through a crack in the hen house. Hundreds of armed soldiers passed through the area.

Then a huge cannon was towed by tractors and positioned in their front yard. Puzzled, Matilda watched as soldiers loaded and prepared to fire the cannon. She counted more than 100 men as they stuffed their ears and noses with cotton and moved away—far away from the beast. Matilda tore the egg basket liner and stuffed her and Max's ears and noses as the soldiers had done. And then, from a long distance, the cannon was triggered. The noise was unbearable, and Matilda and Max both passed out. When they came to, the soldiers and the cannon were gone. The children stayed in the hen house for several days before venturing out to see that their town was reduced to rubble, and its people were gone.

There was more, but Dorie's father could not read further as his eyes filled with tears.

Fear gripped the Britannia Beach community for days. Uneasiness was reflected in their eyes as they awaited the next steamship, their major link to the world. When the vessel docked the steward and the captain were sober and dispirited.

The steward apologized for lacking some of

the ordered supplies. "You wouldn't believe the shelves in North Vancouver! They're almost empty from the hoarding frenzy."

The captain added, through clenched teeth, "The line-ups of men wanting to enlist are long and slow. My son is among them."

That evening Rob was expected and Dorie was helping her mom with dinner preparations. Her father came into the kitchen.

"That pot roast smells delicious!" he announced as he put his arm around his wife's waist and kissed her on the cheek.

"Doc says I'm not fit for warrin', sweetheart. I'm too fat, too slow, and too old. So don't you worry any more."

Dorie's mom turned and held him close, then said, "I can't make you younger, old dear, but I can put you on a diet!"

" … ah, next week, Sweetheart, next week," and he picked up his pipe and went into the parlor to wait for dinner.

A tear rolled down Dorie's cheek. She knew. She knew. A knock on the front door sounded, and Dorie flew to let in Rob. His step was light as he handed her a bouquet of meadow flowers, grabbed her waist, and twirled her around the tiny hall.

"I smell pot roast! My favorite dinner!"

Donny tramped down the stairs.

"Rob's here!" he announced happily, and the family evening was full of chatter and happiness.

After Donny was tucked into bed, and Dorie's father offered to help with the dishes, Rob and Dorie were alone in the parlour.

"Jules," began Rob.

"Don't say it!" cried Dorie in panic.

"I must go; you know that. You have another year of school and can't marry until you're a little older, and I'm having a hard time not absorbing you into my very soul …"

In the silence he could almost hear Dorie's tears drop onto his shirt.

"Just think. It makes sense, Jules. I'll go help put an end to the invasion and be back for your graduation, and we'll get married after your birthday in September."

Dorie lay her head on Rob's shoulder and wept. She felt his tears on her hair. They sat together a long time. Finally Dorie raised her head, fumbled into her pocket for a hanky, and dried Rob's eyes, and then her own.

"I've made your shirt all wet," said Dorie apologetically.

"Doesn't matter, Jules."

"Promise me you will return!" said Dorie.

"I promise. I'll be careful. This conflict will be short; I'll be back before you know it!"

Dorie thoughtfully weighed the situation. "I'll write and work hard in school to make you proud."

"I'll write, too, and I'm always proud of you, Jules. I'd be extra proud of you if you could be brave enough to see me off when I leave on the Britannia."

"When?" whispered Dorie.

"Tomorrow."

"I won't let you down," promised Dorie.

The next morning, dressed in her pink prom dress, Dorie waved her handkerchief at the Britannia steamship until it was out of sight. She felt hollow and dizzy. She lowered her arm and felt the supporting arm of her father. He led her from the docks, gathering a tearful Flo, who had bid farewell to Charlie, and they returned to town.

A few weeks later Charlie returned. He was disappointed and little ashamed that he had been rejected for service. He had a hearing problem and flat feet, and had not passed the physical.

Flo was relieved and assured him he would be helping his country from home.

School began. Dorie threw herself into her studies, and wrote to Rob, stacking the letters until she had an address to send them to. A letter from Rob gave her his military address and she sent a reply immediately, scented with a drop of her mother's perfume.

The letters then flowed, and Dorie felt a little more confident. She noticed with a small smile that Rob's first letter was written while he was on the train crossing Canada.

2. Letters Flow

Rob gazed down the aisle of the train. There were so many men, he thought, I wonder what their chances are in battle. I can't write that kind of thinking to Dorie. What can I write? Dorie likes animals. I'll write about the dog and maybe make it funny.

* * * * *

Dear Jules,

The train is full of eager men. Everyone feels the same, that is that we'll beat the Huns and be back in Canada soon. We pass the time playing chess and poker; I prefer chess's intrigue.

We stop often to take on more passengers—most of them men heading for the war. There are plenty of people at the stations cheering us on. A surprising passenger is a dog that belongs to Andrew McPhail who visits his pet in the mail car. His dog is heading for war service, too. I wonder what a dog could contribute to a war?

Entertain troops, by jumping through hoops?

Dress like a clown, to turn frowns upside down?

When the battle gets risky, he'd bring us some whiskey!

I haven't seen the dog, yet, but I'll bet he's got courage.

I'll find out more later. I hope your studies are going well. I miss you already.
  Love, Romeo

* * * * *

Flo was working in the Britannia grocery store and spending her free time with Charlie whenever he could get down from Camp Jane.

Seeing Dorie one day Flo said, "Charlie and I are going to build a house in Mount Sheer and get married when it's ready. There's going to be a whole town up there!"

"I'll miss you," said Dorie.

"Don't worry so, Dorie. Rob will come home soon and you two can move up there too! It'll be great!"

But Dorie couldn't stop a bit of envy creeping into her heart because she was between letters from Rob and felt so alone. She gave Flo a weak smile and nodded in assent as she said softly, "Yes, someday."

Dorie helped her father in his dry goods store; she helped her mother clean the house; she helped her brother Donny with his schoolwork and did her own homework and checked it twice. No amount of busy work kept the empty feeling away.

And then there was another letter from Rob.

In the dim light Rob looked around the barracks

at the snoring men. Most of them weren't accustomed to physical work and were exhausted. The orientation lectures tried to prepare the men for what to expect and they were therefore scared. Even the issue of uniforms made their purpose more real. Rob considered, "I mustn't tell Dorie anything that will cause her to worry. What can I write?

* * * * *

Dear Jules,

We were whisked through Toronto so fast there was no time to shop or even have a lemonade! We were taken directly to military camp where we were issued boots and uniforms and so on. Fitting the boots took a long time. Maybe they should call it Boot Camp—Ha Ha! Then they put us through training. I suppose it's important to know how to salute an officer but I hope I don't have to stand at attention and salute in the middle of a battle!

I wonder if they're teaching Andrew McPhail's pet dog to salute. He's evidently been cleared for service. He must be a talented pooch. Maybe he is billed to entertain the troops!

How's the weather in B.C.? It's raining here; one fellow says it's an omen, but he's always so negative the men rather avoid him. I miss you.

Love, Romeo

* * * * *

Rob's next letter came soon after the last one and appeared to be mailed from England. Dorie took a breath of relief; Rob was safely in England. She tore open the envelope and read.

* * * * *

Dear Jules,

We sailed from Halifax a week ago. I'm learning the fine points of chess from Lewis. I like that game a lot! We'll have some fine evenings by the fire playing chess, you and I, when I return.

I met Andrew walking his dog on the deck today. The dog's name is Digger and he is a trained rescue dog like the St. Bernards. Maybe he does carry whiskey! He is a black Labrador retriever and follows every command that Andrew utters. Maybe you and I should get a lab someday. Andrew tells me they're a great breed with children.

Love, Romeo

* * * * *

Dorie discovered another letter in the same envelope.

* * * * *

Dear Jules,

We are safe in England. I'm sending this as soon as I can because I'm sure that you'll hear sad news about the English Channel.

Our voyage was blessed with crisp clear weather and we were lulled into peaceful voyage activities. But the captain warned us to be prepared as we neared English waters that the German U-boats are active in the channel and around England and Ireland. We're waiting to disembark at the docks now and grateful that we made it through those threatening waters. Others weren't so lucky. A merchant ship was attacked by a submarine u-boat just ahead of us. Our captain stopped to pick up survivors at the peril of his own ship and all of us. The survivors looked so pitiful clinging to debris, who could not stop? So this is war. It's sobering but it won't stop us. And it won't stop me from coming home when this job is done.

I love you, Romeo

* * * * *

3. Mother Nature Strikes

One evening Dorie was studying for an exam at the kitchen table. Her mother came in and put the kettle on.

"Would you like a cup of tea, Dorie? Oh...oh... oh..h..h!"

Dorie's mom steadied herself by holding onto the table. Dorie's pencil rolled onto the floor. Dishes rattled in the cupboard. Dorie carefully stood and held on to her mother. Gradually, the vibrations and shaking stopped.

Her dad came in, "What the devil was that? An earthquake?"

Alarm spread throughout Britannia as people checked for damage, but it wasn't until the morning that the disaster was known. A landslide had wiped out Camp Jane. Frantic digging followed, but to no avail. Fifty-six people had been killed, including Charlie.

Flo stood stoically with her parents at a massive funeral service. Dorie put her arms around her dearest friend. Flo didn't cry. She whispered, "I can't stay here. I have to go. You understand, Dorie?"

"I understand," Dorie said, as she felt a new emptiness take hold of her. As fragile as it was, she felt her courage crumble.

4. The Funny Thing About War ...

Rob walked away from the mess hall still chuckling about the sense of humour of the Tommies, as the English soldiers were affectionately called.

"No wonder the officers are so stern when they have to deal with such off-hand wit," thought Rob. "It's too raw for Dorie's delicate ears but maybe I can write some of it."

At the barracks he began to write.

* * * * *

Dear Jules,

We were whisked straight off to more military training in England. It was just as well we were taught to salute; the English officers demand the protocol. We were issued guns and spades, mess kits, and tin hats that they call "Battle Bowlers." The hat has a round crown and a flat rim, but it doesn't resemble a bowler hat, believe me. We were taught how to dig with the puny spade for the benefit of the office workers but I certainly know how to dig from farming and mining. Then they showed us how to use a rifle. I had no trouble shooting because I'd had plenty of practice keeping down the prairie dog population in Alberta. I can surely see that the Brits have a well-developed sense of humor. The

Tommies call the rifle's bayonet a toothpick. How can we carry all this stuff and fight too!

Time for lights out.

I love you, Romeo

* * * * *

Spring came and went. Dorie stayed away from the dance but graduated from high school in June, 1915.

Rob wrote little of the war unless it was good news. His next letter, however, made her heart pound as he had his orders and was finally going to the war zone.

* * * * *

Dear Jules,

We have received our orders so we'll soon be in France. I'm writing this now to ensure you receive a letter in good time. I don't know how efficient the mail service can be maintained from a war-zone.

The fighting seems to be centered around Ypres so we'll probably cross to Flanders. Lewis says that the town was once called Leper because it sits on the banks of the Leperelle River. It was the center of the cloth trade. I marvel at Lewis's vast knowledge.

I also continue to be amazed at the British sense of humour. We have a British officer assigned to us and he calls Ypres, a French word that sounds like

"E-Pray," Wipers!

The soft rain of England reminds me of B.C. I hope all is well with you even if it's raining.

Love, Romeo

ps: The prairie boys are anxious about crossing the channel because the Brits claim it's always rough and they're afraid of being sea-sick. Not me! I'm watching for U-boats!

Love, Me again.

* * * * *

Dorie anxiously waited for Rob's next letter to be sure they made it safely across the channel. She waited for three weeks.

Rob stared at the dirt wall of the trench.

"So this is war," he thought. "It doesn't give much time to write a note home to tell Dorie I'm still alive. But I'd better give her some idea of the reality we face."

* * * * *

Dear Jules,

We arrived at base camp already weary from the trek in to our location. We travelled by foot and sometimes by wheels if we were lucky. The base kitchen provided a hearty stew for us and then sent us off to the trenches to relieve those at the front who have been fighting for weeks without a break.

Marian Keen

*Our first assignment was to relocate a section so we
had to dig a new trench. We added an underground
room and are being teased about our "parlour"
but we find it a comfort. Keep those letters coming.
You wouldn't believe how much assurance letters
provide. The boom of canons and the whine of
bullets is unnerving, but we keep our heads down.
It's getting colder and these socks are too thin.
Murray says his socks are already full of holes. He's
a big fellow; I guess his feet are big too and put a lot
of strain on the socks we were issued. We asked for
more but so far no luck! It's raining.*

Miss you,
Love, Romeo

* * * * *

Rob flinched at a close explosion. His unit was
under a barrage of fire and they were hunkered
down patiently waiting to reciprocate. At least it
was daylight. He pulled out his writing kit.

* * * * *

Dear Jules,

*We're back in the trenches; we had a good break
at base camp. We expected a rest but were put to
work. I was assigned to kitchen duty and peeled
mountains of potatoes, and onions and carrots and
turnips. I unloaded the farm truck yesterday. I was*

glad I knew a bit of French. The old farmer seemed grateful to the fighting men. He has lost a son to the war. The French farmers are doing their best to feed all the soldiers.

Lewis and Albert are working for the platoon newspaper called "The Wipers Times," and many men write articles for it. Some of them even write poetry. Believe it or not, I decided to try to rhyme a bit just for fun. This is what I wrote. I call it "Our Cosy Little Parlour."

We dug our trench on orders first,
In pouring rain we felt a thirst.
We made a place to give relief,
Quiet and dry beyond belief.
A room to have a cup of tea,
Remembering civility.
It was our parlour in the trench,
Others laughed and mocked and hence,
We sipped our tea and played some chess,
Forgetting war, and all its mess.
Now gunfire whines and canons boom,
While comfort fills our tiny room.
With candles lit we sit on rocks,
And change our wet and dirty socks.
Once refreshed we join the fray,
Ready to fight another day.

Others who once mocked our room
Now seek its comfort from war's gloom.
Our parlour steels us to the core,
And so we're going to win this war!

I was quite surprised to find they printed my effort in rhyme in the "Wipers Times!"

Lewis and I created the parlour. There's no more teasing. Now, everyone uses it.

Murray joined the "Y-players who put on skits and vaudeville. Murray is a big guy so they cast him as a woman wearing a string mop for hair which is good because he hasn't any—hair, that is. In the skit the new bride (Murray) is looking at ads in the Wiper Times for property for her hubby to build her an ivy-covered cottage.

The bride reads, "Located between Plug Street and White Street the foundations have already been dug and the land cleared of all foliage for the landscaping of your choice. "No man" has a lien on this property and it has a lovely view of Wipers. Act now; this property is in great demand from opposing bidders."

Laughter sure relieves a lot of tension. We enjoyed our so called 'rest' back at camp, but it's back to business now.

Love, Rob

* * * * *

Dorie noticed his closing was scribbled as if in haste at the bottom of the page. And she missed his signing off as "Romeo."

5. Dealing with Anxiety

Dorie held the bedpost ... smoothed her pink dress ... dabbed pink on her lips ... perfume ... the Schottische music ... twirled ... fell into a ditch ... mud on her pink dress ... gunfire ... cannon ... BOOM!

She woke in a sweat. Her head ached. She reached under her pillow. Rob's letter crackled. He was still okay. She lit the lamp and put on her robe. She wondered why did he sign Rob instead of Romeo?

She began writing, "Dear Rob, please send your next letter to Flo's address in West Vancouver. I am moving there to find work."

She could hear her mother in the kitchen. She finished her letter and went down to break the news to her parents. In a few weeks she boarded the Britannia. It was a relief to be taking action. Dorie waved to her parents and Donny on the docks. Dorie couldn't wait to see Flo, who assured her that work was waiting for her. Flo had room in her cottage and would appreciate help with the rent.

And Dorie was grateful not to be in Britannia to see another graduation.

Flo's cottage was half-way between the ferry building where she worked, and Dundarave where Dorie would work for Miss Jessie at the Clachan.

The Clachan was a small hotel on Dundarave beach which was always fully booked in the summer.

The two girls soon fell into a pleasant routine. Up early to breakfast together, then off to work; Flo on her bicycle to the ferry building where she sold tickets, and Dorie walking to the hotel where she cleared breakfast dishes, made beds, and helped with lunch.

At the end of their work day they listened closely to the BBC news on Flo's wireless. Then after a quick bite of dinner, off they went to the Women for the War Effort meeting.

As the war continued the newscaster's voice sounded grim as he listed the ongoing battles and casualty statistics in a monotone. The numbers of dead and wounded kept climbing.

500,000 Armenian citizens executed by Turkish authorities.

Canadian nurse Edith Cavell executed for helping fleeing soldiers.

U-boats sink neutral ship Lusitania off the coast of Ireland.

After months of dwelling on the news from the war, Dorie's dreams became vivid and frightening nightmares. Once again she was dressed in her pink frock. She was trying to apply lipstick using a shattered piece of glass. She heard Rob cry out to her. She followed his voice through a dense green fog. Was that Rob ahead in between pillars of rubble? "Get down, Jules!" he shouted. Dorie tried to duck and tripped on her long skirt and fell and kept falling … "Help! Help me, Romeo …"

"Wake up Dorie! Wake up!" Flo, dressed in her fuzzy flannel robe, shook Dorie's shoulder.

Dorie woke with a shudder. Flo sat on the bed and put her arms around her friend. "You're having a bad dream, Dorie. It's not real."

"But the war is, and it has invaded my mind."

"Canada's sent our best men," said Flo. "They'll turn the war around, you'll see. Things will get better."

6. Face to Face, it's Murder

Rob was having his nightmares, too, but his were real. He sat in the trench and trembled.

Today, he and a team of sharpshooters had been ordered to clear Kitchener's Woods. German snipers occupying the woods had targeted allied soldiers fleeing the deadly gas that spilled down the hill into the trenches. Rob had witnessed the men who made it back to base camp coughing, then collapsing in wretched spasms as they lay dying.

Rob had been eager to stop the slaughter but approached the trees with caution. He remembered every detail. Albert had shimmied up a tree and was spotting the enemy snipers from his high perch. But a German trooper had spotted Al and was moving through the bushes to get a clear shot at him. The trooper was now only four feet from Rob but unaware of Rob hidden by a tree trunk and some low growth. As the German raised his rifle to take a shot at Al, Rob spurted out from his cover and caught the man's torso with his bayonet. The man fell to the ground with a look of surprise and anguish contorting his face.

Rob couldn't stop reliving the horror of taking a man's life like that. It felt like murder, not target shooting. He tried to think of Dorie to keep a hold on his sanity. He pulled out his writing kit and thought of her, trying to picture her as he had danced with her. He held her hands as he nodded off looking into her blue eyes. They twirled around, but then her eyes changed to those of Donny's and the twirling went on as they moved to more shallow water. Then again the blue eyes changed to those of the German soldier whose face grimaced as he fell to the ground. Rob called out, "Jules!" and woke saying her name over and over. He took out his pen.

*　*　*　*　*

Dear Jules,

We went for a walk in the woods today. It smelled refreshing and spring-like. Albert showed quite a talent for climbing trees and Murray was envious, I think. Murray's not very nimble and can't even lift his own weight. He has lost a bit of weight though, so maybe there's hope that he'll be an athlete yet! Al picked up a stray dog that was hiding in the woods. The poor thing was starving, but Al has been sharing his biscuits and dried beef, and now the dog follows Al everywhere and is even learning some tricks. Al calls him Axle! The dog is brown. Why not call him chocolate? But Al builds automobiles so why argue with his choice.

What do you think about our getting a dog?

Love, Romeo

* * * * *

7. Girls Soldier On

Dorie grinned as she lowered Rob's letter and caught Flo's eye as she looked up from her knitting.

"He's okay. He wants us to get a dog."

"Great idea!" said Flo, "I like dogs!

"Me, too!" said Dorie and added, "Especially labs."

"I like collies," said Flo.

"And poodles!" ventured Dorie with a grin.

"And bulldogs!" added Flo.

"And great Danes!" laughed Dorie, "But they eat too much."

"Don't worry about that," said Flo. "Dogs eat anything. We'll collect scraps from our neighbours!"

"Where would we get a dog?" asked Dorie.

"If it's meant to be, one will turn up!" said Flo positively.

The girls returned to their routine.

The next day at breakfast Dorie asked, "How many socks have you made, Flo?"

"I haven't checked, but we're getting low on yarn. I'll purchase some when I visit Betty. I guess we should take what we have to the war relief."

"No, let's send what we have directly to Rob for him and his buddies, and let's tuck a cake into the package."

"A cake! It wouldn't keep."

"I have a recipe. Miss Jessie gave it to me. It's called war cake. It won't spoil and it gets better with time, she says."

"Let's try it. I'll get the ingredients after work and we can bake it tonight. Maybe we can cheer up the men at the front."

But the mail took time and it was many weeks before they knew whether their efforts were a success. Finally a letter arrived from Rob.

Rob wiped his tears with the back of his hand as he peeled onions for Cookie. Rob's mind continued to dwell on the coughing he could hear from the hospital tent. More men had been gassed. This time with mustard gas. How could they fight when they couldn't breathe?

Al threw a turnip into the vat with a clunk. "Sarge says our gas masks come today," said Al. "He also told me they're bringing fans from England. Would you believe a woman invented a fan that will clear the trenches of gas?"

"I would," said Rob. "Women are amazing! Just think of Marie Curie and what she's doing, bringing x-ray equipment to the front herself! Talk about courage! Did Sarge know the name of the woman?"

"He did. She's Hertha Ayrton and by a strange co-incidence she's a friend of Madame Curie's. Uh, oh! Cookie's calling!" said Al, "and we'd better get these to him or our names will be mud."

"That's all we need, Al, more mud!"

The mail truck rolled in as they came out of the mess tent. Men swarmed around Rob as he received a huge package. Someone produced a knife and the cake was divided and eaten in a blink. Rob cleaned up the wrappings and carefully tucked the last of the cake and a pair of socks into his pockets. He was glad that Al and Lewis and especially Murray were able to grab socks. He thought, "Must write Jules and Flo."

In the middle of said task, Rob had just written,

… and my friends were also lucky to receive your wonderful, unholy socks, especially Murray. Thank you. The cake has a fantastic flavour. I saved a piece for later—selfish I guess.

The grind of the supply truck interrupted his thoughts. He left the tent to see what was up. The usual supplies had already been delivered that morning. Men were again unpacking boxes and joshing over the contents.

"They're gas masks, guys, look at me!"

"You'd scare your own mother to death with that, Bud!"

"Let's go scare the germs!"

"Don't bother! They're not scared of nuttin!"

"At least we can breathe!"
A while later Rob continued with his letter.

We had quite a spell of laughter when we tried on our gas masks. We looked like google-eyed creatures from another world. We were lucky that our unit wasn't in the field that was gassed. I also learned that a lady invented fans to clear the trenches of gas. Anyway, now we're prepared!

Our courage is doubled when we eat cake! YES—that's a hint. Thank you with kisses from all the boys, but especially from me.

Love, Romeo

* * * * *

8. What Else Can We Do?

1915 ended and 1916 began, and the war raged on. Rob's letters were less frequent. Dorie and Flo put their heads together to invent new ways to help the war effort.

Thinking of the packages they'd sent, the girls discussed the things that worked and those that failed.

Flo said, "The cookies shattered, the brownies dried up, but the war cake held up. According to the WWE, toiletries, warm underwear, and socks are needed. I'm going to the city to see Betty and I'm on the buying committee to purchase some of those necessities. Meanwhile, we've knitted and sewed, baked, and collected money for the war effort. What else can we do?"

"We'll think of something different; we should think up an idea to keep the soldiers' spirits up."

In the evenings the girls listened to the wireless. It was a dark and rainy evening in February when they listened to the sounds of fire from the war. Some brave and crazy reporter had recorded the Germans attacking France.

"Will this war never end?" pondered Dorie frowning in her frustration.

Flo was frowning too as she stared into the little

flames in their fireplace. "It's so awful," said Flo. "And here we sit by our cozy fire while they're in mud-frozen trenches trying to stay alive. I can't even imagine how it must be. The soldiers must be going quite mad."

Dorie nodded, "It's unthinkable."

"Yes-s-s-s," said Flo soberly, "it is. But it's given me an idea!"

She turned to Dorie. "You write regularly to Rob. What do you write about?"

"Just stuff. What I'm doing, who I've talked to, the weather. Boring stuff—why?"

"Exactly! And yet Rob appreciates your letters. It's news from home no matter how boring; it's what their fighting for!"

"So what are you suggesting?"

"What if we wrote to every soldier in Rob's unit. If Rob could give us his commanding officer's name we could get the first name of every man in the unit and write stories in individual letters addressed to Joey or George or Timothy at the unit address and then write inside "Dear Beau" and end with "Your friend Jane." Flo ended breathless, "What do you think?"

Tears glistened in Dorie's eyes. "Flo, that's brilliant and so caring, so compassionate. Let's begin with the names we know—Albert, Andrew,

Lewis, and Murray. I'll write Rob for his CO's name. This is something we can do!"

Creativity flowed and blossomed with more ideas. Dorie wrote about the snowdrops blooming in the neighbour's yard. Flo wrote about about the first robin to arrive. And the project took every minute they could spare and every cent for postage they could scrape up as the list of soldiers grew. They shared their idea with the WWE and even more letters flowed overseas.

One day in March, it was freakishly sunny and warm. Flo took her lunch and her writing kit to the beach to start on another letter. She opened the hinged wooden box to retrieve pen and paper and began with, "Dear Beau." With sandwich in one hand and pen in the other she was thinking of what to say next when she looked into the warm, begging eyes of a young pup; his honey-colored fur covered pitifully protruding bones. Flo fed him from the rest of her sandwich. His tail wagged with gratitude. Flo gave him a pat, finished her lunch and went back to work.

When her day was done she stepped out the door into rain, and paused to raise her umbrella. A thumping sound drew her attention. The pup's wagging tail banged against the side of the building.

"C'mon, pup! There's more food at home and I

don't like to walk alone. My bike has a flat tire so that makes it a long walk. It's nice to have company."

When she arrived at the cottage she opened the screen door and ordered the puppy, "You stay!" She opened the door to a tantalizing aroma; Dorie was in the kitchen.

Flo called, "Smells good. What's for dinner?"

"Shepherds pie!" Dorie answered, and walked out of the kitchen.

"I hope you made lots. We have a dinner guest," said Flo.

Dorie nodded, "Sure, who?"

Flo opened the door wide, "Dorie, meet my new Beau; he seems to have adopted me." She turned and said to the puppy, "It's okay. You can come in now."

The puppy ran past the girls and into the kitchen.

Laughing, Dorie said, "I think you bribed him!"

"A starving puppy? What could I do?" Flo grinned.

Dorie said, "He's lucky he met such a softie!"

Flo countered, "He loves me; he's my Beau!"

"Lucky Beau," said Dorie, "Nice name."

Flo improvised a bed from a crate and towels, and placed it by her bed. Fed and bathed the puppy went to sleep.

"We'll have to check for his owner," said Dorie.

"I know, but isn't he sweet?"

When the girls could find no trace of the pup's owner after several weeks, they stopped looking. Lucky Beau had found a permanent place in their hearts.

To earn his keep the pup lightened their thoughts of war and gave them plenty of stories to write to the soldiers overseas.

9. When Will it End?

And the war went on. The newscaster sounded less than human as he flatly listed battles and casualty statistics. The battle of Verdun began in February 1916 and continued even as another battle began in July—the battle of the Somme—which stretched over thirty miles at its front.

"Will the war never end??" was on everyone's lips.

And the casualties mounted higher and higher.

Late in the fall it began to rain and the soldiers had even more disasters with transport, discomfort and disease. From the onset of winter to early spring it looked like whichever side "could survive" would win the war.

The girls continued writing to the soldiers, but Rob's letters became rare. Finally Dorie received a letter in late spring.

Rob woke after four hours of sleep. The tunnels would soon be complete after weeks and weeks of laborious digging. Lewis was such a hard worker and he was the best at setting explosives. Just a few more days of work were required to finish the tunnel. Perhaps this will give us an edge, he thought, and pulled out his pencil.

* * * * *

Dear Jules,

I've been reassigned, and my Britannia talents are now useful. Lewis volunteered to work with me, so I've come to know him quite well. Back home he was a history teacher, so that rather explains his vast knowledge. He's quick, strong, and smart. We confer about life after the war as we work and I'm certain that I'd be happy teaching kids. Will you be happy married to a teacher? I promise not to be a stuffy one!

Thanks for the letters you and Flo are sending to our unit. They help keep everyone's spirits positive. You're doing a great service.

I miss you so much.

Love, Romeo

* * * * *

That was the last letter Dorie received from Rob.

Dorie continued to write to Rob and to other soldiers as well, but it was hard to remain positive wondering why Rob didn't write. Was he still alive? If something had happened to Rob, the authorities would notify his family. Did they know about her? How would she ever know?

She read and reread Rob's letters but continuing

nightmares haunted her night and day. She had dark circles under her eyes from lack of sleep.

Gently but firmly Flo said, "Dorie, you have to take care of yourself. Rob will need you when he returns."

"If," said Dorie.

"You haven't received any notification. Rob is just busy and tired, I'm sure."

"But they'd tell his family, not me!"

The newscaster continued reporting statistics and reported that heavy rains were hitting the front lines. Then one day, December 6, 1917, he sounded rattled. With a trembling voice he reported an explosion in the Halifax harbour. Two ships had collided; one had been shipping armaments to the war zone. Later reports in the following days told of 1600 dead, and 9000 injured. It was the biggest explosion ever known.

On New Year's Eve, Flo hosted a little party to keep everyone's spirits up. At midnight she gave a toast, "Chin up everyone! It's 1918!"

Everyone raised their glasses of punch.

"To the end of this bloody war!" said one.

They clinked glasses and drank. And the "bloody war" continued to take its toll on the living.

Marian Keen

In April, 1918, the BBC reported the Red Baron had been shot down by a Canadian pilot.

In August, the radio reported a major battle in Amiens. Canadian troops had broken the German defences.

Flo hugged Dorie, "The war's turning!"

In September, Canadian troops broke the northern part of the Hindenburg Line, and by October, Canadians had captured Cambria.

On November eleventh, the church bells rang and rang. Horns tooted and people shouted. Flo and Dorie ran to catch the newscast. Even as they ran, people stopped them for a hug. Their neighbours waited on their porches to share the news. It was truly the end of the war to end all wars. And the tears ran.

Life returned to a dull routine. It was almost a year since Rob's last letter, and there was still no word. Dorie struggled to accept that she had lost Rob and all he'd promised. Then she made a decision. She would save every penny for more education. She would earn a teaching certificate for herself and carry on teaching children. In this way she would honour Rob and his hopes for the future. It seemed fitting, and gave her purpose.

Dorie visited her family for Christmas. Her father thought well of her decision, and gave her a little seed money toward her education fund.

The New Year brought new resolve. As Dorie was free of war effort volunteering, she now worked in a dress shop during the day and waited on tables in the evenings. Flo remained in her job at the ferry building, and life went on.

10. Courage

Dorie grasped the bedpost … dabbed pink on her lips … the music of the Schottische pulsed in her head … she twirled to the waltz and ran down the path as fast as she could. She fell, and woke up crying. And life went on in spite of recurring dreams.

It was almost February, 1919. Crocuses were pushing up through the ground around the little dress shop. Mrs. Williger insisted that she could wear the blue dress that she admired on the hanger, because she'd bought the same size last spring.

"A little too much celebrating the end of the war," murmured Dorie to herself as she tried to interest the woman in another blue dress, and kept her finger over the size.

Back at the ferry building, Flo was dealing with a room full of passengers who had just arrived on the ferry and were seeking shelter from a downpour. Flo waved an envelope through the window at Billy, the boy who ran errands for her.

"Billy, run over to the dress shop and get Dorie. Tell her to come here to me, and tell her it's a matter of life and death! Hurry!"

Billy ran.

Billy burst into the dress shop. "Flo wants you

right now. She's in trouble. She said it's life or death. Hurry!"

Dorie turned to Martha who was learning the business. "Martha, Mrs. Williger will take the blue dress. Her change will be $2.20. Wrap the dress in tissue. I have to go. It's an emergency!" And Dorie ran down Bellevue Avenue, through the rain to the ferry building to save her friend!

The building was jammed. Dorie pushed through to the ticket counter at the south end. There, leaning on the counter, was a red-haired, freckle-faced man still in military uniform. He was flirting with Flo!

Dorie flushed in anger. "This is life or death?"

Flo nodded. "It certainly is, Dorie. Meet Andy. He'll explain this," and she handed the envelope to Dorie.

Dorie read "Miss Dorothy Sanders," before the envelope was snatched out of her hand by Andy as he pointed the way across the room with it. "I addressed the envelope. Flo said you are Miss Sanders. I'll give it to you in a minute, but first I have a job for you," said the redhead as he pushed and pulled her through the crowd.

Bewildered and stumbling, Dorie echoed, "a job?"

"Yes. It was a big explosion from Big Bertha. Shell shock, you know." Andy stopped. "Please get this fellow on his feet and thinking straight again. I've been his caretaker since we met again in a Belgium hospital. He's obsessed about some treasure. All he can say is 'jewels.'"

The man sitting on the bench raised his head at the word, and Dorie looked straight into Rob's blue eyes.

"Jules," he said, and rising to his feet he took her into his arms.

Andy took a quick intake of breath and let it out slowly as he watched Rob and Dorie embrace. "So … you're Rob's treasure; you're his 'jewels.' I should have guessed it was someone's name. Many of the injured cling to or focus on someone they love."

Dorie sat on the bench next to Rob. She said quietly, "It's J-U-L-E-S, short for Juliet, my middle name. My pet name for Rob is Romeo because his middle name is Roman. It's just sentiment with a touch of humour. Was it a problem?"

Andy nodded, "Just that all we had was an envelope made out to "Miss Dorothy Sanders" in his pocket. His identification and everything else including any possible letters, disappeared on the way to the Hoogestat Hospital. My dog Digger found Rob under a pile of rubble in Passchendale. The clean-up crew dug him out while Digger and I looked for more casualties. Then later, Digger and

I were injured and by chance he and I ended up at the same hospital. I stayed on at the hospital to help out because I could do a lot there, but I couldn't return to my assignment because Digger needed more time to recover."

"Rob wrote me about your Digger. Is he all right?"

"He's fine but he couldn't get on our ship, so I'm waiting for him to get home. Meanwhile I'm making sure Rob is looked after."

Dorie was full of questions. "Tell me about Rob. He's so quiet!"

I'll be happy to, Dorie, but first, is there a restaurant nearby? We're starvin' hungry!"

"Oh! Of course! It is late. Come to our cottage. I'll make some sandwiches."

The rain had stopped, the crowd had gone, and Flo had finished for the day, so the four of them walked to the cottage. Rob walked slowly, hesitantly. He watched the ground apprehensively, but he held Dorie's hand firmly. Dorie's eyes filled with tears as she realized that Rob wasn't quite himself.

11. Andy's Story

Flo warmed some soup and made some sandwiches as Andy explained.

"Rob and I first met on the way to England. We continued to meet now and then because we were both assigned to the Ypres area. The war was very intense there as you probably know. Digger and I had the task of locating the dead and the wounded.

"The first time I encountered Rob was after the Ypres gas attack by the Germans. Rob was a sharpshooter and was assigned to the unit to clear Kitchener's Woods of German snipers. The Germans were positioned to overlook the fields full of gas victims and were shooting anyone who moved. After the woods were cleared, some of our boys didn't return, so my crew and I were assigned to recover them. I found Rob crouching by a tree suffering from the shock of his first hand-to-hand combat. There were many men that I encountered in my mission that had the same emotional shock after killing the enemy close enough to see their eyes. That part of war is hard to cope with, because the obliged action is against their code of ethics and moral fiber. I know it was so with Rob because he kept saying to me, "Did you see his eyes? Did you see his eyes?" So I went over and closed the dead man's eyes. It was a terrible shock to Rob."

Dorie clearly recalled Rob's words. "We went for a walk in the woods today. It smelled refreshing and springlike." She wiped her eyes with the back of her hand as it began to dawn on her that all of Rob's letters had pointedly protected her from the horrors that he had had to face. Andy paused as Flo handed Dorie a handkerchief and he asked her "Do you want me to continue?"

"Yes." Dorie said, "I need to know as much as you can tell me."

"The second time I found Rob was after he had been assigned to the 177 Tunnel Brigade. He and Lewis worked three of the many tunnels to place the massive explosives that would undermine the dug-in German forces. Coming out of a tunnel, Lewis sprained his ankle and they didn't make it to the safety and protection of the trenches in time. They were knocked off their feet with the tremendous impact of the explosion. Even people in base camp were knocked to the ground. People twenty-five miles away thought it was an earthquake. The docs said Rob and Lewis had "shell shock." Rob had headaches after that for a few weeks, but he knew his name and he seemed okay so he was reassigned to clear the town of Passchendale of lingering enemy. The Germans were still blasting the town to rubble, so there would be nothing left of it. Finally all was quiet, so Rob's unit was ordered to go in. Rob was one of the first men into the town. But there was one more blast from the Huns' Big Bertha cannon from the far edge of town. It was aimed at the last chimney still standing—the chimney toppled, burying Rob in its rubble.

"Some time later my unit went to check the town, and Digger found Rob. My boys uncovered him. He was babbling a lot and raving incoherently about some jewels and then he said quite clearly, 'It's important not to panic in tight situations.'"

Dorie nodded at the words.

"And then he passed out and was carted off to the hospital. We continued to sift the town for more casualties. It was a treacherous landscape and both Digger and I got caught by more falling stone. Digger broke his leg and I broke my arm, so we all ended up at the Hoogestadt Hospital. I stayed on and helped out a bit at the hospital because I was officially a dog handler so I waited for Digger's recovery. It took a while. Digger was more injured than they thought at first but he recovered eventually."

Dorie watched as Rob finished his sandwich. His hand shook as he ate his soup but he managed it all.

He never said one word as Andy talked. Dorie put her hand on his arm; "Rob, have you had enough to eat?"

Rob nodded and patted her hand.

Andy said, "He finds talking difficult, but the doc says his speech will return to normal."

"Is there any other injury?" asked Dorie. "I noticed he has difficulty walking."

"No," Andy smiled. "Just shell shock said the doc. It jars the brain and it takes time to recover. Rob was bruised a bit, but that's cleared up. I'm his speech."

Andy studied Rob and Dorie as they sat gazing at each other. Andy coughed slightly, "I could use some fresh air?"

Flo said, "Lucky Beau needs a walk."

Andy and Flo quietly left for a stroll on the beach with the dog. As they walked they planned what steps needed to be taken.

"Shouldn't his family be notified that he has returned alive?" asked Flo.

"Yes, of course. Now that I know his identity I can obtain the information. I'll do that," said Andy.

"And he'll need some clothes," said Flo. "I'll see to that with Betty's help."

"Who's Betty?" asked Andy.

"A relative of mine in Vancouver who is

resourceful and gets things done."

Andy and Rob took rooms at the Clachan. Andy joined the fire department and hoped to set up a rescue service for the North Shore. A much thinner Digger finally arrived to do as he was best trained to do.

Every evening Andy and Flo walked the two dogs along the shoreline and it wasn't long before friendship grew roots.

Rob was able to take a job at the local grocers and he gradually began to speak. The days grew longer as spring approached.

Every evening, Rob and Dorie walked along the beach to watch the sun set over Vancouver Island. Dorie asked Rob no questions at all, either about the past or the future. She refrained from any pressure that might disturb him. She confined her thoughts and spoken words to their present activities.

But one day Rob received a letter. He handed it to Dorie.

"Read please. It's from my parents. I should answer. I don't know what to say."

"Do you remember them?" asked Dorie.

"No." Rob bit his lip and frowned.

"Don't worry, Rob. I'll help you write your reply. You can confess to a fuzzy memory and say you look forward to seeing them soon. All noncommittal until you do remember … and you will. We'll write tonight, okay?"

"Oh, Dorie. Thank you. You always make me feel comfortable." And Rob hugged her.

12. A Question on the Beach

It wasn't long before Rob nervously handed Dorie another letter.

"My mother is planning to visit. She asks when. She has to make plans. She will come by train. She needs a place to stay. What can I do?" Rob looked upset.

"Oh, Rob, that's wonderful! Don't worry so. We'll write back and put it off a little, while you adjust to work and make the needed arrangements. Your mom will understand. I can't wait to meet her. And we're in the rainy season yet so we'll fix it so she comes in warmer weather."

Time passed and the days grew longer as spring approached. One evening, Dorie was chattering away as they strolled, telling Rob about the Britannia landslide, the loss of Charlie, and the move to West Vancouver to join Flo. She thought Rob wasn't listening because he did not respond to any of it.

"Jules … Dorie … " said Rob, and stopped.

Dorie stepped back and faced Rob who was still holding her hand but was now down on one knee.

"Marry me." said Rob.

"Yes, oh yes!" said Dorie, "but not until you kiss me!" And she pulled him to his feet. Dorie and Rob walked slowly back to the cottage hand in hand. Andy and Flo had returned from walking Beau and Digger, and were sitting on the porch with the dogs.

Andy stood and said, "Time to get you back to Miss Jessie's for your beauty sleep, Rob. Work starts early!"

Rob nodded. He said, "True. But first, I asked Dorie and she said 'yes!'" Rob lifted Dorie's hand and kissed it.

Flo clapped her hands. "How wonderful! You both have waited so long, you deserve every happiness!" and Flo hugged Dorie and then Rob.

Andy kissed Dorie on the cheek and then shook Rob's hand. "But you still need your beauty sleep, old friend. It's getting late."

"Yes," said Rob. "I know. Much to do. Need rest, but … I'm happy!"

Dorie took Rob's face in her hands and kissed him. "I'm happy too, Romeo! Have a good sleep, I'll see you tomorrow."

Rob and Andy waved good-bye and walked to the Clachan.

13. Obstacles

Dorie and Flo took the dogs into the cottage. Once inside Flo took Dorie's hand. "Tell me about Rob's proposal. When did he pop the question? Where were you? Did he propose on his knee? Did he kiss you?"

Dorie laughed. "On the beach; at sunset; on his knee; and yes!"

"Oh Dorie! I'm so happy. You've waited so long, all through that horrible war."

"Yes, yes I did." The smile on her face faded into worry.

"What?" asked Flo. "What's wrong?"

"Nothing's wrong, Flo. I love Rob, and I want to marry him. It's just that …"

"What?"

"It's just that nothing's right!"

"What's not right?"

"Well, not everything of course. I love Rob and we're happy and Rob's finally talking and he even has a job … but …"

"But?"

"We have obstacles."

"Like?"

"Money to pay for Rob's education. Rob isn't fully recovered, and he'll need to be well to earn his teacher's certificate. Who should study first? Will I ever teach? I do have my heart set on teaching. And where will we live after we're married? Way over in Vancouver? We'll have to find a rental. And moving away from you to a new, strange area. And enrolling for school in September? That's only a few months away. And on top of all that, arranging a wedding? Where will we have the ceremony? And meeting Rob's parents? And having my family come down from Britannia, and what to wear?

"Stop!" laughed Flo. "You're wearing me out! You're making mountains out of ant hills! And you're not alone, Dorie. You have me, and your parents, and surely Rob's parents will want to see him soon. They'll be so excited to meet you! And of course there's always my Aunt Betty!"

"Your Aunt Betty? She's your aunt? I thought you'd made her up!"

"Made her up? No! She's real. Why did you think I made her up?"

Dorie gave a little shrug. "I thought you just said that as an excuse to do a little shopping in Vancouver!"

"I'd better explain my Aunt Betty," said Flo thoughtfully. "First, she insists I call her 'Betty' and leave off the 'Aunt' because it makes her feel old otherwise. She's very well off, and I'm her 'poor niece.' Every now and then she nags me to visit her so that she can buy me something. That makes her feel charitable, and makes me feel like I am her poor niece! Most of the time she is so involved with her charities that she ignores me, which is a good thing. Then once in a while she has nothing to do, and thinks to herself, 'charity begins at home,' and she insists that I come for a visit to my poor lonely aunt's and she takes me shopping and for lunch. Mom says I should humour her because she is all alone. But Betty's pretty eccentric you understand."

"I see," said Dorie.

"And I don't talk about her much because it doesn't make me feel good about myself when I see her. But now, I see she could actually be helpful, Dorie, for you. She has connections, and loves to help people. She could easily find you and Rob a place to rent, and provide a recommendation for you on your school application without lifting a finger. She would thoroughly enjoy the activity, and it's not charity. She's just someone who knows how to get things done. That's why I thought of Betty."

"And why would your Aunt Betty want to do this for me? She doesn't even know me. I'm not a poor relative."

"Because you're my best friend. I love you, and

admire you so. At my lunches with Betty I talk a lot about you. It started when you first came down from Britannia Beach and I told her you were coming. She wanted to know all about you, so every visit she asks about you. Betty has a good heart and she really cares. Believe me! ... There's just one thing ..."

"And what's that?" asked Dorie.

"She's really eccentric."

"In what way?"

"First and most obvious is the way she dresses. She's colour blind, so her combinations can be ghastly. Remember, she's very charitable. So at the beginning of the war she was so shocked by the cruel invasion of Belgium, she contacted friends of her deceased husband in Europe. 'Send me two of those poor Belgians. I can employ them and give them a home.' Believe it or not, a young woman and her 12-year-old brother arrived a few months later. She'd already forgotten, but was delighted. She put the young woman to work as her housekeeper, and the boy she turned into her purple-clad butler. And they love her!"

"How did she come by her money?" asked Dorie.

"She married a rich, older man. He died, but the interesting part is that he had invested in railroads, and made a fortune. She sold that investment and continued investing in other enterprises. She has a talent for making money. But she herself lives frugally. Believe it or not, she even buys some of her clothes at a second hand store. She spends her money on everyone else. She's strange."

Dorie said, "She sounds quite lovely. And fun. When can I meet her?"

"As soon as you tell your parents, and Rob tells his parents. Then Betty can be told, and we can visit with her. I'll arrange it; she'll be delighted."

"Thank you, Flo. I feel relieved already," said Dorie.

"Good. And Dorie, don't worry about getting your teaching certificate first. Betty is a suffragette and she believes that women should be encouraged to use their brains, and you certainly have a good one! And, you said it yourself, Rob is really not ready to start his education. He needs time to adjust to normal life. So, my dear friend, you have to put yourself first, and get your certificate. Then you can help him get his. And … with that thought, we'd better get to bed!"

"Yes, Mom!" Dorie said laughing. "I think you're the smart one!"

"Yes, thank you daughter!" Flo laughed. And no more nightmares! That's an order!

14. A Friendly Situation

The moon was rising as Rob and Andy walked back to the Clachan.

After a moment Andy said, "Congratulations, Rob."

"Thanks," said Rob.

"Just a touch premature," said Andy.

"Can't let Dorie down. Five years ago I promised," said Rob.

"But you're not ready, Buddy. How can you support her?"

"I need her promise."

"You already had it; she waited for you."

"No date set."

"Rob, think Buddy. Now that you've asked, Dorie won't want to wait anymore."

"I saved. My war pay will come. We'll manage."

Andy dropped the subject, and turned his thoughts to his own situation.

The next day, as they walked Digger and Beau, Andy and Flo exchanged thoughts on their friends. Both of them felt responsible for Rob and Dorie because they cared about them.

Andy said, "Thank goodness I ran into you at the ferry office. You helped me identify Rob and Dorie."

"Tell me again, Andy," said Flo. "Why didn't you know exactly who Rob was?"

"Well, I knew his first name was Rob from when we all rode the train across Canada on our way to the war. And I saw him again on the ship to England. But being a dog trainer, I spent most of my time with Digger and the dogs, more than the men.

"Even though I located him on three different rescue missions, our relationship was casual. I knew his first name, and had my crew transport him twice to the medic tent at base camp. At Passchendale he'd been buried a long time under rubble before Digger found him. I was impressed that he hadn't panicked in that tight situation, but passed out once he was found. Because he was unconscious, we sent him to the hospital at Hoogestadt. My medical crew dealt with urgent emergencies and moved fast. Their aim was to save lives. Sometimes personal belongings and even ID was lost in transport. Can't blame them. And Rob was a volunteer on that mission, so the others clearing out Passchendale only knew his first name.

"I did know that Rob was from British Columbia, and that he'd volunteered for dangerous missions. The nurses found the envelope addressed to Dorie with your address in West Vancouver in his pocket. I was returning to BC anyway, so ..."

Flo said, "Rob's speaking has surely improved

since he returned. He's speaking in sentences now. Do you think he's well enough to continue his schooling?"

"Not quite. His speech is better, he walks better, but he has gaps in his ability to remember. The Flemish doctor said that memory loss could be expected, but would likely return in time."

Flo nodded in understanding and then said, "Dorie wants to further her education and obtain her teaching certificate. I told her to go ahead first, and give Rob time to recover."

"Good advice. They need time. Rob is lucky that he got a job at the grocer's. I think that work has helped him recover his speech. And of course Dorie has helped tremendously. They sure have a strong love. I'm beginning to understand what love is, and how powerful it can be."

"You can see it in Dorie and Rob," added Flo. "Yes, it has been strong enough to survive a war."

"Not only them, Flo. I'm feeling it myself."

"Really?" Flo looked at Andy, with questions and surprise in her eyes.

"Yes," said Andy, "and I have a hunch you feel it too."

The colour rose in Flo's face. She said, "Oh...h, uh ... "

And Andy took advantage of the moment and

kissed Flo long and hard.

Beau and Digger were far, far ahead by the time the two of them became conscious of their surroundings, and that they were not alone on the beach. Other strollers couldn't help but smile at the kissing couple.

15. Wedding Plans

Replies to Dorie and Rob's letters to their parents were prompt. Dorie's mother wanted to make Dorie's wedding dress and planned to come to Vancouver to purchase the materials. Her letter was full of suggestions and support.

Rob's mother's letter reiterated her intention to visit in August, before harvest time on their farm. She was eager to know if Dorie and Rob had set the date.

In a separate letter to Dorie, she expressed concern about Rob, 'I understand Rob lost his memory. Does he remember his family yet?'

Dorie said to Flo, "It must be painful for his mother to think her own son doesn't remember her. Surely he will soon. Maybe he needs to see her. What shall I tell her?"

Flo said, "Just tell her that Rob is living in the present. And suggest that reminders of his family and life on the farm would really help, so when he actually sees his family it will all fall into place. And Dorie, now is the time to set the date and place. Then I'll contact Betty."

The two girls grinned at each other and began to plan the wedding.

Dorie said, "Rob's mother wants to come in

August, and I hope to be in school in September so I guess we must choose a day in August. Rob's brothers and sisters, and Donny will enjoy the beach. I love the beach. Rob proposed on the beach. We should be married on the beach."

Flo said, "Why not the beach by the Clachan? Miss Bessie would make a lovely luncheon, I'm sure."

"That would be perfect. Rob would be comfortable there, and so would I. But would she be booked up now?"

"It's still early Spring. Let's go see Miss Bessie. She'll give us good advice."

That afternoon the girls walked the dogs to the Clachan.

Miss Bessie checked her calendar. "The second week in August is almost clear. So I could accommodate everyone except for the first weekend. But I have an ace up my sleeve" her eye's twinkled with mischief. "I've been urging Mrs. Miller to open a guest house. She lost her husband in the war and needs money, but she's not very sure of herself. This will convince her. If we could juggle the overflow on the weekend and send you and Rob there for your bridal night."

By the time the girls left, the arrangements were made and the date was chosen for the wedding.

In her excitement, Dorie wanted to tell Rob how wonderful everything was working out, and that evening as they walked on the shoreline she laid out all her plans for the wedding. Then she hit a major obstruction—Rob, himself.

"We cannot marry this August. Too soon."

"I thought you wanted to marry me. You asked me!" wailed Dorie.

"Too soon. My war pay hasn't come from the war office. I need it to support you and for my education."

"But Rob, I have it all worked out. I'm going to normal school in September. I have the funds for that. You can work in Vancouver and then I'll work while you go to school the following year.

Rob became agitated. "Wives don't work. I will support my wife. My wife will not have to work! A woman's place is in the home!"

Dorie's face was taut with anger. "And what do you think I've been doing for the past four years? I've carried two jobs and as I've said, I've saved enough to go to school too. I'm not just a weak, little kitten that needs feeding and petting. I'm a fully grown woman and I can do whatever it takes!"

And with that declaration of independence Dorie turned her back on Rob and stormed back to the cottage.

Rob stood on the sand dumbfounded, unaware that the surf had covered his shoes. "What happened?"

16. Adjustments

Andy and Flo were walking the dogs when they came across Rob still standing in the water on the shoreline. Dorie was nowhere to be seen.

"Uh oh!" said Andy. "Something's gone wrong; Rob's in shock."

"Where's Dorie?" asked Flo.

Andy handed her Digger's leash. "I'll see to Rob. You go to the house and find her."

He hurried across the sand to the waterline and couldn't resist the habit of his war job as he scanned the water for Dorie's body. He gently guided Rob up the beach and kept his voice calm as he said, "You got your feet wet, old buddy. We'd better get you back for some dry shoes."

Andy hailed a passing car, and the driver was kind enough to drive them to the Clachan.

As Andy put Rob to bed, Rob said, "I lost her, Andy."

Andy didn't have to ask who. "How so, Rob?"

"She ran away from me. She doesn't want to be my wife. She wants to be a teacher and work! She even cut her hair. She's not the same anymore."

Andy sat on the bed. "Think, Rob. Remember the nurses at the hospital? They fed you; they helped you walk again. Think of the girls who drove the commanding officers' trucks. Think of Marie Curie who delivered x-ray equipment to the front. Think of Hertha Ayrton who invented the trench fans. There were women who worked the farms so we could eat. There were women who worked in factories making bullets for our guns. Dorie wasn't in the war, but she worked two jobs and still found time to knit socks, bake cakes, and write to you and your unit. Dorie is accustomed to looking after herself. Think, Rob. You haven't lost her. She's just grown up! And she still loves you, you lucky dog! Not all veterans are so lucky!"

"But she's planned the wedding for August. It's all arranged. And she wants to go to school in September to become a teacher," protested Rob.

"So she's a capable woman. You should be happy she's not just a pretty face. Did you really want to put her in a cage and feed her and pet her?"

"But she ran away from me!"

"What did you say to her?"

"I said I could support her. No wife of mine is going to work!"

"Rob, get some sleep. The war changed everybody. We all took on grievous responsibilities, and now we're all older. Tomorrow you go to Dorie and apologize. You were wrong, and you're lucky to have such a wonderful, capable woman."

And Andy turned off the light.

"Andy?"

"Yes, Rob?"

"Why haven't I received my service pay from the war office?"

"You were already paid, Rob."

"I was paid a few francs for spending money, yes, but I mean the regular pay," said Rob.

"You must have filled out a form which you've probably forgotten about. Most soldiers gave directions to send their pay to their closest relative. Who might that have been, Rob?"

"I guess it was my mother."

"She'll have it safely put aside for you, I'm sure. Have you asked her about it?"

"I'd better do that," said Rob.

Andy left Rob to think and sleep on his advice, and thought to himself that Rob is finally coming out of his fog. As he stepped into his own room, he wondered how Flo was coping with Dorie's reaction.

As Flo approached the cottage Beau began to whine. Then Flo heard Dorie crying. Her first thought was at least she's safe. Flo let the dogs into the cottage, and followed the sounds of crying coming from Dorie's bedroom. Beau bounded in to see Dorie, and comforted her in his own doggy way. Digger followed, sniffing to be sure she was okay, and then lying down quietly as trained.

Flo put the kettle on for tea, and armed with a wet washcloth and a drink of water went into Dorie's room, put her arm around her friend, and said simply, "What happened?"

Dorie pushed Beau away as he tried to lick her face. She wiped her face with the warm washcloth and had a sip of water before she said, "It was awful. We had a fight. Rob doesn't respect me. We can't get married if he doesn't respect me, can we? He doesn't want to get married anyway. He wants to wait until he's rich so he can support me like a china doll. He doesn't realize I'm a fully grown, capable woman—not a child!"

"What did Rob actually say?" asked Flo.

"He said August is too soon; he hasn't enough money to support me. He said no wife of his was going to work and he said I didn't need to teach, that he would be the teacher and support me; that a woman's place is in the home."

"I see," said Flo.

"What am I going to do? The wedding is arranged. I'll have to cancel everything!"

"Don't be so hasty, Dorie. Give Rob a chance to think about what you want. He'll want to please you, I'm sure."

"But the wedding!" cried Dorie.

"There's time to adjust before then. Remember you were only 17 when Rob went to war. He still thinks of you as 17. He dreamed of you for all those war years, but he didn't realize you were growing up."

"I suppose," said Dorie.

"And," added Flo, "Rob returned unable to communicate. From what you tell me he spoke in complete sentences tonight and expressed his thoughts and feelings. That's a big improvement. So now you can work it out together. Without proper communication you went ahead and made all the arrangements. So it's quite a shock for Rob when he's probably still thinking he has to protect you like he did in his letters."

"Yes, he did, didn't he?" said Dorie.

"You know, Dorie, the Great War changed everything and everyone. Andy and I have talked a lot about it. But you and Rob avoid the subject, and it's not helping either of you adjust. Both of you have lost five years in your relationship. You can't expect everything to be normal in less than two months. So you need to show your mature ability to understand Rob, and his recuperation. And apologize to him."

"You're right. I didn't get my way, and I acted

like a kid with a tantrum. I'll apologize right now!" and she stood up.

Flo pulled her back to the bed. "Time enough for that tomorrow. Let Rob sleep and think and you do the same. Night!"

And Flo went back to rescue the kettle that had boiled dry, and went to bed. As she drifted into sleep she wondered how Andy coped with Rob, and whether Rob could adjust to life after war.

17. Sharing the Good and the Bad

Dorie turned over her egg timer for her soft boiled eggs and raised the sides of the toaster. Flo had already left for the ferry building. Digger had been taken to work by Andy.

There was a knock at the door, surprising Beau who was asleep under the kitchen table. Dorie mumbled to herself, Who comes knocking at such an early hour? She pulled the sash tighter on her robe, and hurried in bare feet to answer the door. It was Rob.

"I'm sorry!" they said simultaneously and fell into each other's arms.

Egg timer emptied. Toast burned. Eggs boiled dry. But all was ignored by the two responsible adults as they were occupied with more important activity. Beau whined as the smell of burnt toast filled the kitchen.

Eventually a loud bang drew their attention and Beau barked in shock. Coming from the bedroom, Dorie and Rob laughed at the ridiculous mess in the kitchen. Dorie handed Rob a potholder and he moved the burnt pot into the sink and filled it with water. Dorie removed the blackened toast and tossed them in the trash.

"I'll boil some more eggs," giggled Dorie.

Rob chuckled. "We'd better get dressed first in case your neighbour investigates the sound of the gunshot!"

"Right! Those eggs made quite a bang!" laughed Dorie. "By the way, aren't you supposed to be at work?"

"I told them I had an emergency, so I'd be late."

"Guess what, Rob. I think you're late."

"Another minute won't hurt," and Rob kissed her again.

Minutes later Dorie had eggs boiling in a spare pot, and bread toasting in the crumb-free toaster. They grinned at each other across the table as they ate.

"Dorie, I could never confine you in any way," said Rob. "You are too valuable to me; clipping your wings is unthinkable. I'm actually so proud of you I'm bursting. To think that you want to teach children as I do. Your plan is sensible. What is the first step? Have you applied?"

"Not yet, but Flo's been helping me plan, and we're going to see Betty, and she has agreed to help."

"Betty?" asked Rob.

"Yeah. That's where I went wrong, Rob. I should have shared how I came to make those decisions instead of sparing you the stress of making decisions. The truth is, I was afraid of telling you anything that might upset you."

"The only thing that upsets me is the thought of losing you. We're past that now, so let's share our problems and decisions. So tell me, who's Betty?"

"Betty is Flo's eccentric aunt. She is well-to-do and loves to be charitable."

"We don't need charity!" said Rob emphatically.

"No, we don't, I agree, but according to Flo, Betty has connections through her charitable work. She could find us an inexpensive rental, and is also able to recommend me for normal school entrance. That's why Flo is taking me to meet Betty the day after tomorrow. Betty is a connection I can't ignore, and Flo has spoken of me so often that Betty wants to meet me. What do you think?"

"Wow! All that good sense from the teen-aged sweetheart I left behind. I'm impressed. But don't accept charity."

"I won't. Unless she buys me a hat!"

"A hat?"

Dorie laughed. "As I said, she's eccentric. Flo says every time they go for lunch Betty has to visit her favourite hat shop and buys a hat, if not for herself for anyone else she fancies. So there is that danger."

"She sounds frivolous."

"She does, doesn't she? On the other hand, Betty

also brought two war refugees to Canada and employs them and looks after them. She loves to help people."

Rob said, "While you go see Betty, I'll contact my mother and find out if she spent or saved my army pay."

"Rob, your thinking and speech have cleared," observed Dorie.

"Yes. Except for my memory. There seem to be gaps. I'd better get to work."

"Me too," said Dorie. "Leave the dishes. I'll look after them later."

And with one more kiss for the road, they began their day.

18. A Little Eccentric

Two days later Dorie and Flo set off to see Betty. Flo tied a kerchief over her red hair; Dorie followed her lead and they were glad for the precaution. It was windy in the inner harbour. Once ashore, they caught a jitney to take them to the south side of the city, and walked two blocks to Betty's house on the Crescent.

Dorie was unprepared for the size of it. "She lives in a mansion!" she said to Flo.

"I told you she was well-to-do."

"I know, but …"

"Stop gaping, Dorie! Oh my goodness! She never ceases to amaze me!"

Dorie followed Flo's gaze. Two gardeners were stooped over on the side of the driveway. They stood up at the sound of the girls. One was a youth, about 15; the other was a rather stout looking woman wearing light blue overalls, boots, gloves, and a huge sunhat. The overalls didn't quite contain a yellow garment that protruded above the waistline. As the woman rose, Dorie saw her hat had a hole in the crown and a huge knot of flaming red hair exploded out of the top.

"Morning, Betty!" said Flo. "I'd like you to meet my friend, Dorie."

"Oh my goodness! I thought Max and I would be finished by the time you arrived." Betty removed her gardening gloves, stepped over the plants, and extended her hand to Dorie. "I'm so glad that I am meeting you at last. From what Flo says, you want to teach children. I approve. I want you to meet my friend, Max."

The young man stepped over the plants, shook Dorie's hand and said, "Pleased to meet you, Miss. Good morning Florence," and returned to his work.

Betty said, "Max and I are almost finished. Just run up to the house, Flo, and ask Tilly for tea. She made scones just for you girls and she's proud of them. I'll be there shortly. Aren't these marigolds lovely? Their bright blue flowers will be so soothing in the heat of summer!"

Flo guided Dorie up the drive before she could say a word. At the door Flo rang the bell. She smiled at Dorie and said, "colour blind."

Dorie nodded in understanding.

The door opened. Dorie's eyebrows rose.

"Miss Florence. Happy to see you. Come in," said the young woman.

"Hi Tilly," said Flo. "I can see you've been baking."

"Special treat for Miss Florence. You like tea now?"

"That would be lovely, Tilly. This is Miss Dorie Sanders, my good friend."

Tilly extended a hand tinged with flour, and a little flour blew like puffs of smoke from the spring breeze off her white chef's attire, complete with baking hat.

Dorie suppressed a giggle as she shook Tilly's hand.

Tilly didn't notice as she beckoned them in. "The parlour is ready for you; I bring you tea for two." And she hurried into the kitchen.

The parlour was large and amply furnished with comfortable chairs. Dorie and Flo sat by the window to enjoy the view of the North Shore mountains. They waited and idly chatted for more than ten minutes.

"Clearly we were a little early," said Flo with a smile.

"Doesn't matter," said Dorie. "This is a pleasant place to wait."

"Bump!" went a side door as Tilly entered with the promised tea. Gone was the baking outfit. Tilly was now dressed as a proverbial French maid—black dress with white cap and apron above her white baking shoes and socks. She curtsied and served tea and scones to the girls and left.

A minute later Betty walked in, looked at the tea

served, and poking her head through the side door, hollered, "Tilly! You forgot the clotted cream!" She smoothed out the wrinkles in her yellow skirt that had evidently been forced under the overalls. She was much smaller than she first appeared to be. She took a seat and poured herself a cup of tea.

"Now, my dears, tell me where you're at with your plans and I'll tell you the steps I've taken."

Not knowing what steps Betty had taken, Dorie felt at a loss, and looked to Flo.

"The most important information is that Dorie and Rob are getting married in August," said Flo.

"Ohhhh! I love weddings. What can I do to help?" asked Betty. "Are you marrying your soldier, Rob, is it?"

"Yes," smiled Dorie. "We're keeping the wedding simple and small, and it's arranged. But both of us have decided to attend normal school with the hope to teach children. We will stagger our attendance. I will attend the first year, and Rob will work. Then, while I teach, Rob will attend. This means that we'll need a place to live for about three years. Would you know of a modest rental close to the normal school?"

"Perfect!" said Betty. "As I said, I took steps, that is, I inquired. I strongly recommend Mrs. Smith. Widowed, left with a huge house, she's had difficulties renting it out because of people's stupid prejudices. So how biased are you and your fiance against German Jewish people?"

Dorie paused, "Mrs. Smith is German?"

"Yes," said Betty. "She and her husband left Germany long before the Kaiser started making trouble. Her husband was a business man, did well, and bought a big house. When he died some years ago, she altered the house to rental apartments and did well until the war. You see, her name was really Sarah Klaus, but when the war began her house was regularly pelted with rotten tomatoes. She changed her name to Smith to help stem the hate. It hasn't helped and she has difficulty renting."

"Does she rent to couples?" asked Dorie.

"Yes. In fact she has a big apartment on the third floor complete with kitchen. And to your benefit, a trolley runs straight to the normal school."

"Can I meet her? Can I see it?" asked Dorie.

"Slow down Dorie, you'd better ask Rob first," said Flo.

"We'll call him on the telephone. Where would he be?" asked Betty.

"He's working at the grocery store now," said Dorie. "But he'll be at the Clachan later this afternoon."

Betty said, "We'll finish our tea; tell Tilly how

tasty her burnt scones were; go shopping; see Mrs. Smith; and call Rob. Oh! I forgot. Here are the application forms for normal school. I fortunately got two copies in case you smudged the ink, but if you're careful Rob can make out the second one for the appropriate year. I've signed both. Are we ready? Let's go buy something fun. How about a hat? And we'll stop for lunch!"

Dorie sat overwhelmed. Flo pulled her to her feet, saying, "I told you to just go along with it. You'll enjoy it." And they followed Betty to her car.

Dorie whispered, "Betty drives?"

Flo nodded. "Like an expert."

Later that same afternoon Tilly once again served tea in the parlour. Dorie and Flo were worn out after following Betty around town all day, and were grateful for the chance to relax. Non-stop-Betty was in the hall on the phone to the Clachan. They could hear her side of the conversation clearly.

"Hello? Is that you, Bessie? How are you doing, my dear?"

"Oh good, glad to hear it. Yes, I'm well too. I'm calling to talk to the bridegroom, Robert Chase. I understand he's staying in your lovely inn, and that the wedding will take place there?"

"Yes, it's perfect for them."

"Yes, I have enjoyed my visits there too."

"Yes … you're catering it too?"

"Oh, I'm sure Helen will do a lovely lunch. If there's anything I can do, you can call me."

"Yes …"

"Yes …"

"Yes, I'd like to speak with him if he's there …"

"Tilly! Could you bring me a cup of tea? In the hall?"

"That's a dear, thank you."

"Hello? Is this Robert Chase? This is Betty. Your fiancee and my niece Florence are with me now."

"Yes, we've had a lovely day together. Rob, I rang to get your opinion on a very delicate matter. I hope you will find no offense in my query."

"Yes … I have found a decent accommodation for you and your lovely bride while you attend normal school, but to put it bluntly, the landlady is a German Jewish widow, and I want to know if you, as a former soldier would be offended by that."

"No? … Ha ha ha … I see why Dorie wants to marry you!"

"Yes, Dorie met her and viewed the apartment this afternoon. She loves it … yes …"

"Thank you, Rob. I look forward to meeting you too. Thank you again. I'll book it right now."

Betty stepped into the parlour.

"What did Rob say? asked Dorie.

"About the landlady, he said there was no bias on his part because he fought in the war to stamp out that kind of prejudice. He added that he hoped she wouldn't be offended by his inherited blue eyes and Irish sense of humor. And about the apartment, he says he trusts your judgment completely. Now that's a real man for you."

"I think so," said Dorie, blushing in pride.

"Good. Now that's done, I'll phone Sarah and book it for September, and then we'll have supper and talk about the wedding some more before you must ferry back to the North Shore. Isn't this fun? I hope Rob likes your new hat!"

19. Family Shopping

Spring was heating up promising a warm summer. The four young people worked as required but spent their free time exploring the rugged terrain of the North Shore. The girls packed picnic foods and the men planned the hikes. The great outdoors and the exercise it demanded produced rosy cheeks and increased stamina. Rob was almost back to his old self, which was fortunate because his mother couldn't wait for summer to visit.

One day, Dorie and her mother were studying sketches of wedding dresses that Betty had supplied for the project. The sketches covered the table, some chairs, and even the floor when there was a knock at the door.

Dorie scrambled to clear her lap of pieces of fabric, and sketches, and her pad for notes when the knock was repeated.

"Coming!" she called.

She opened the door. Rob stood on the porch. A woman in a blue suit and hat held his arm as if she owned it. She looked at Dorie with a smile.

Dorie looked at at her deep blue eyes and said, "Mrs. Chase, what a wonderful surprise!" She reached out and Rob's mother moved quickly to embrace her soon-to-be daughter.

Dorie's Mom was there in a blink, and the two women were friends without hesitation. Chatting, they moved to the table to look at the sketches.

Rob put his arm around Dorie and said quietly and proudly, "She's my Mom."

Dorie said, "Do you really remember her?"

"I really do. Wow. How could I have forgotten her and Dad?"

"It doesn't matter, Rob. You have that memory back and you are so much better. Let's make tea. I have some biscuits, cheese, and jam. It'll give us all a chance to get to know each other. Though," Dorie looked at the two women bent over the table, "I think they already do!"

As Rob passed the table he glanced at the scattered papers. He said, "Dorie, I know wedding dresses are white, but could you add a little pink for old times' sake?"

Dorie giggled. "Rob, you remember the strangest things!"

"You, in pink, are unforgettable!"

"I promise I'll keep that in mind."

Before they finished their tea, Flo arrived, and Mrs. Chase and Mrs. Sanders asked Flo for directions about shopping in Vancouver. Flo was fairly familiar with Vancouver, but finally she said,

"I will arrange for a shopping guide of the finest ability. I'll call Betty."

Two days later, early in the morning, Dorie and her mother, and Rob and his mother were met at the ferry by Betty in her car. She drove almost as fast as she walked.

Their first request was to visit some furniture stores. Under Betty's guidance, two stores were visited, and the first purchase was made within an hour. Happily overwhelmed, Dorie and Rob picked out their bedroom furniture.

Rob's mother said, "This is a tradition in your father's family, Rob. We received our four-poster bed from your father's parents, as they were given theirs. This will be your first wedding present, I believe, and Betty has arranged for delivery to your apartment on the first of September.

Dorie hugged her soon-to-be mother-in-law, and she and Rob thanked her sincerely.

Betty strode towards them smiling broadly. "Beautiful choice, well done. Now Rob, I asked for your time this morning especially, as I have a surprise job interview for you, and we have just enough time. I've called your present boss, and he's agreed, and is recommending you for the position. I'll explain as we go. So back to my automobile, ladies, no time to waste!"

In the car Betty said, "Your interview is with the supervisor at Woodward's Department Store. They are expanding, with a new grocery department, and need staff and managers and you have an excellent opportunity."

Betty dropped Rob off with advice for the interview and directions for his return to the North Shore. Dorie gave Rob a kiss for good luck. He walked away with a spring in his step, and she thought, what a difference.

Rob's mother said, "Rob looks very well, dear. It must be the sea coast air!"

"You must be very proud of your son, Mrs. Chase," said Betty. "From what Dorie and Flo have told me, Rob is a true war hero."

"I am proud of Rob, yes," replied Rob's mother. "And I'm also so relieved that he remembers me and his Dad. His friend Andy has accounted for so much about Rob's service. I had no idea. He wrote, of course, but one would think he had experienced a walk in the park on a spring day compared to the ugly truth of war."

Dorie's eyes glistened as she put her hand on Rob's mother's arm and said, "That's what he wrote to me, too. He was protecting us."

Mother Chase patted Dorie's hand. "I expect Rob

will soon learn you're made of stronger stuff than one would expect from such a delicate, lovely girl, as you are!"

As she parked the car, Betty said, "Well, ladies, on that serious note, now we're going to have some fun!"

Dorie looked out the car window at the Hat Shoppe, and laughed.

Almost two hours later they left the Hat Shoppe smiling, Betty and Dorie leading the way, arm in arm. The two mothers, flushed with pleasure, carried hat boxes which contained special hats for the wedding. Betty had had her fun again.

The rest of the afternoon was full of various shades of white silk, lace, and pink satin. The three returned on the ferry laden with packages, tired and very content.

20. Retrograde Emotions

Part way into June the weather turned hot. It was a good time for salads, hot dogs on an open fire, lemonade, and barefoot strolls in the cool Pacific water. One evening it turned muggy and hot. Flo, Andy, Dorie, and Rob sat on the cottage porch sipping lemonade. The dogs were restless and started to whine.

"What is it Digger?" asked Andy. "I haven't seen you this nervous since ..." Digger pressed his body close to Andy's leg and lay his muzzle on his knee.

Beau pawed Flo's lap for assurance. Flo petted his head and stroked his ears. She looked out over the Strait of Georgia to Vancouver Island. There was a flash of light.

"It's an incoming storm. Dogs always get nervous with storms," she said. "But the rain will cool things down and clear the muggy air."

They watched as the storm approached. Forks of lightning filled much of the sky. The flashes became brighter as they grew closer. Tympani rumbles followed the flashes.

"Look! The lightning is peach and pink," said Flo. "I've never seen that before!"

"CRACK!" a closer bolt on Point Grey lit up the sky.

The dogs whimpered. Andy and Flo brought the dogs inside where the two canines scrambled rapidly to Flo's bedroom and hid under her bed.

Andy partly closed the door to muffle the sound of the storm. Flo closed her window and drew the curtains. They returned to the porch to watch the spectacle.

Andy glanced at Rob as another bolt cracked, and was followed shortly by a big BANG! Rob jumped. He crushed Dorie's hand in his, and sweat broke out on his forehead.

Andy gestured to Flo as another bolt hit with a sudden clap that shook the cottage. As rain thundered down, gusts of wind blew it onto the porch.

Andy pulled Rob to his feet and said lightly but loudly, "C'mon gang, let's make some popcorn." They went inside to escape the blowing rain and the chill of the storm.

Flo lit candles. Andy filled the popcorn maker and set Rob to shaking it over the stove. Dorie melted butter and she and Andy made more lemonade.

Another flash lit the cottage; the crack of thunder immediately followed, jarring the very floor. Rob stopped moving. Andy gently but firmly moved his arm so the kernels wouldn't burn. And Rob nodded, returning to the job at hand.

As the storm moved east and up, over the mountain the four took bowls of popped corn and sat in the comfy chairs, munching contentedly. The rain let up to a steady drizzle, and the storm's muffled rumbles sounded soothing.

Rob smiled. "I did it. I made the popcorn."

"Only a few burnt ones, Buddy!" chuckled Andy.

"I'll open the door," said Flo. "It must be cooler now."

As she did, the fresh air cooled the stuffy room, and the dogs came out to join the party.

"If this rain doesn't stop soon we'll have to walk the boys in the wet," said Flo.

"We have slickers, but not for the canines," said Andy. "Let's wait a bit; see if the rain peters out. Otherwise you'll have the smell of wet fur tonight."

They fed the dogs to put off their walk, and shortly after, when the great storm had finally morphed into peace, Flo and Andy took the dogs out.

The storm left clear weather, and the four friends took full advantage of it during the last care-free weeks of their summer.

Suppers at the Clachan were a treat, but cookouts on the beach were more frequent. One afternoon on the beach, Rob was dozing as Dorie laid out the picnic. Flo and Andy were roughhousing with

Digger and Beau. As the playing grew more frantic the dogs began to bark, and Andy and Flo's voices grew louder as well. At that moment, Dorie bumped a glass jar of pickles against the thermos jug.

Rob roused and sat upright. His gaze fell straight on Andy and Flo, who at that moment were locked in a kiss and embrace. Rob's eyes widened, then frowned.

"Where's Charlie?" asked Rob.

Dorie put down the pickle jar.

She took Rob's hands and held them. "No one told you? Perhaps you've forgotten?"

"Told me what?" asked Rob.

"It's sad news," said Dorie. "So brace yourself."

"Tell me," said Rob.

"Charlie was not accepted for the war effort, so he returned to Britannia Beach to work in the mine. He and Flo made marriage plans, including building a home up at Mount Sheer." Dorie took a breath.

"So what happened?" asked Rob.

"A landslide happened," said Dorie, and choked. "It wiped out Camp Jane and killed 57 men … including Charlie."

Rob let go of Dorie's hand, and dropped his head in his hands.

"Many women lost their loved ones in the war, Rob," added Dorie. "It was too ironic. That's why

Flo left Britannia and moved to West Vancouver. I joined her later."

For a time there was silence.

Shortly after, Flo and Andy approached.

"Not ready yet?" said Flo.

"We can help," added Andy.

"Yes, said Rob. I can see you do help."

Andy looked puzzled by the comment, but Dorie caught his eye and shook her head no. The subject was dropped.

21. The Wedding

The wedding gifts began to arrive, including china, linens, and cookware. One delivery brought a delicate pink vase trimmed with gold. Dorie and Rob opened gifts together. As Rob pulled the vase out of the tissue padded box, Dorie opened the card.

"Oh my goodness! Imagine that!" exclaimed Dorie.

Rob admired the vase. "It reminds me of your dress at the graduation dance. Who is it from?"

Dorie blushed. "It's from Arthur Collins. I haven't seen him since I left Britannia."

"Who is Arthur Collins?" asked Rob. "Do I know him?"

"Well, kind of," replied Dorie. "You used to call him Shorty."

"Well, I was right," Rob grinned. "That fellow Arthur has always had good taste!"

And then suddenly it was August. Carefully and lovingly made by her mother, Dorie's wedding dress hung beneath its dust cover in the back cupboard, over the boxed wedding gifts. Guests arrived. Rob's father treated all to dinner the night before the wedding. Dorie's clothes were packed and placed at the honeymoon bed and breakfast.

Everything was set.

At two in the morning Dorie was wakened by the rumble of thunder from the west. Wrapped in her robe she watched as the storm moved east. As it grew in intensity, Flo woke as well, and joining Dorie put her arm around her waist.

Quietly Flo said, "Rob is okay. He has Andy and his folks there at the Clachan if he wakens. Don't worry, Dorie."

Dorie stifled a sob. "What if he has an episode and stands me up? I couldn't bear it. I've waited so long!"

"Don't cry, Dorie," said Flo. "You'll have puffy eyes for the wedding. And I guarantee Andy will have him there."

The storm grew louder as it neared. The rain began.

"Rain on my wedding day!" fretted Dorie.

"It's good," said Flo. "It'll clean up the beach and be all fresh for the ceremony. Dorie, get some sleep. I personally guarantee that the sun will shine today for your nuptials. Now get to bed!"

At the Clachan Rob was dreaming. The sound of the cannons grew louder and louder. Rob watched the reflections on the clouds to determine the location of the targets. Bullets whined overhead. Everyone huddled in the trenches. A sudden bang panicked Al's dog, Axle, and he leapt and scrambled out of the trench. Al scrambled after him. With a thunderous clap the two of them were caught in the fire, rose into the air, and dropped back into the trench.

Rob sobbed, "No, no, no, not Albert. I saved him!"

"Wake up Rob!" urged Andy. "It's just a storm, buddy. Just another thunder storm."

Rob's eyes opened. "A storm? Where am I?"

"You're close to marrying the girl of your dreams. Jules, Dorie. Remember?"

"Jules, Dorie. My Dorie. How am I so lucky? How could I forget? Oh Andy, I love that girl!"

"I know, Rob. So get some sleep. The storm is over, the war is over, buddy. Just rest."

"Jules. Lucky … love Dorie." And Rob was asleep.

The sun popped up over the mountains in the east and smiled on the sleeping wedding party and guests. Andy's brown eyes slowly opened and focused on the clock sitting on the list of chores he had to do as best man. And all of it had to be done in time for him to drive Mr. Wilson's car over to pick up the bride and her maid of honour. Andy brushed his hair vigorously into confusion, and went to wake up Rob.

At the cottage, one green eye, covered by a lock

of bright red hair, popped open. Flo brushed back her red curls and pinned them. Beau and Digger whined to go out. Flo went to wake Dorie.

"Happy Wedding Day, Dorie! Wake up! We've slept in a bit so we have to move quickly! While you bathe, I'll walk the dogs."

For the next few hours happy chaos reigned. Thanks to the best man and the maid of honour, Mr. Wilson's car driven by Andy arrived at the Clachan minutes before the ceremony was to begin. Andy helped Flo and Dorie out of the automobile. Dorie's Mom, Miss Bessie, and Donny were there to greet them.

"Where's Rob?" asked Dorie.

"Rob's on the beach," replied her Mom, "sitting in the most beautiful arbor covered with salal and pink roses. Rob and Donny made it this morning. Rob is facing the ocean so he won't see you until you walk down the aisle. Here comes your Dad to escort you. Andy and I will go first. Oh Dorie, you look so lovely! Mr. Wilson is here with his new camera. So smile for him and we'll have this day forever!"

Donny took Flo's arm and they followed Dorie's Mom and Andy down the slope to the beach.

And then Dorie was on the aisle on her father's arm.

The beach was crowded with well wishers straining to see the bride. Dorie's father paused as they turned to walk to the arbour. Dorie remembered to smile as Mr Wilson took their picture, and then she saw Rob.

He rose to his feet at the minister's signal, and nearly staggered back into the minister as he first saw Dorie.

"Almighty God," Rob murmured. "Thank you for sparing my life for this moment of beauty and love."

"Amen," said the minister.

And with a sun sparkling sea, and clear salt air, the ceremony of 'I do's' began and concluded.

The onlookers trickled away.

The guests enjoyed a delicious lunch and bridal cake.

And then Mr. and Mrs. Robert Chase drove away in Mr. Wilson's car to their honeymoon nest.

Amen.

22. The Landlady

Two weeks later Rob and Dorie listened attentively to their landlady over tea and biscuits in her parlour.

"War is never over, believe me. I speak the truth," said Sarah thoughtfully. "Since you asked me about Germany, Rob, I will tell you what I know from a personal viewpoint.

"I was too young to care about politics. My father owned a jewelry store, and it did well. I attended a Jewish school, and life was full of dinners at my uncle's restaurant, visits to the park and the museum, concerts, parties and pretty frocks. I was shielded from the rising animosity to our kind. I didn't even know that my father's closing of the store was because the front window had been smashed and the store vandalized by an anti-Jewish mob. I just enjoyed our holiday in Switzerland while the store was repaired. I was 15, and ignorant. I did well in school, however, and by the time I was 20 I had held jobs and was becoming somewhat aware. Then I got a job working for a gentile German business man. He was a widower with a young son. He was a wonderful, thoughtful man, and we fell in love. He was well connected and politically aware that the situation in Germany was not a jolly

Bavarian picnic for Jews, so he met with my parents and offered to take us all to Switzerland.

"My father dissolved his business and we did just that. My father and mother remained in Switzerland, but my husband Hans and I decided to seek a new life in Canada. Hans died of cancer during the war so I am left with his dear son, Stephan, and this big house. And now I have you two to care for," and Sarah smiled as Dorie gave her a big hug.

"So where is Stephan?" asked Rob.

"He lives with me, said Sarah, "but he works very hard, at two jobs. You won't see much of him. We are very fond of each other. Someday he wishes to go to university to study the sciences."

"Commendable," said Rob.

"Yes, I am proud of the boy. Now, how can I help you get settled? Your furniture has arrived, and many boxes. I took the liberty of lending you a small table and chairs."

"Thank you so much. We will unpack and see what's needed. We have another week before Dorie starts school, and I have work. Thank you, Mrs. Klaus.

"Just call me Sarah."

"Sarah it is."

Weeks later, as Rob rode the trolley home from

work, he thought about Sarah's house and how skillfully it was laid out. He and Dorie didn't have to use a narrow, back-staircase but used the grand front one. The main hall was open to all. Two young ladies—a nurse and a hat shop clerk—lived on the second floor, and also used the front stairs. It was homey, and he and Dorie even enjoyed a view of the mountains from their apartment on the third floor.

Rob was walking up the front steps when a slim, young man with blond hair and blue eyes opened the door to come out.

One look at him and Rob could feel the rifle in his hands, smell the fresh evergreen of the woods, and see the splatter of blood as the young German soldier's blue eyes stared in surprise. Rob staggered up the last steps.

Stephan quickly supported him, and helped him to the bench on the front porch.

"Are you ill?" asked Stephan. "Want some water?"

Rob took a breath, patted Stephan's hand, and shook his head.

"No, no, you just reminded me of someone," replied Rob. "I'm fine, thank you."

"If you're sure? … I could get Ma …?"

"No, I'm fine. I was just startled."

Stephan ran lightly down the steps, and then

turned and waved back at Rob.

Rob sat for a few more minutes to let his mind settle, and then went in to see what Dorie had made for supper. To his delight, it was pot roast.

Over supper Dorie and Rob shared their day, and afterwards did the dishes together. Dorie then studied as Rob read the newspaper. Given this time to think, Rob recalled Stephan's features, and matched them in his mind's eye with those of the man he had killed. The similarity was incredible. Rob couldn't help wondering if they were related.

"A penny for your thoughts!" said Dorie, smiling.

"They're not worth that much," said Rob with a weak smile as he shook the paper and returned to the editorial page.

It was late in November when Rob, running an errand after working at Woodward's, found himself on an unfamiliar street near the waterfront. It was dusky dark, and he heard a scuffle and threatening voices up ahead. As he reached the corner, three men scattered through the light of the streetlamp.

"Dirty Hun," shouted one. Another ran past Rob, who had a good look at his face.

Rob scanned the street and there, to his left, was a body on the sidewalk. Without thinking Rob hurried to help. The man groaned and turned onto his back; the streetlamp lit his face. It was Stephan.

Rob crouched down. "Stephan, it's Rob from the house. Where are you hurt?"

"Don't tell Ma," groaned Stephan.

"I won't. Unless I have to. Stephan, where does it hurt?"

"Belly. And m'nose. Ugh!" Stephan wiped blood away from his face.

"We need to find medical help," said Rob. "Can you stand?"

"Yeah. Give me a minute. There's first aid at work and it's close. Help me up."

Rob supported the young man as he rose. They stood for a moment as Stephan adjusted to an upright position. Rob spotted a wallet on the sidewalk. As Stephan stepped away Rob picked it up and then continued to support the young man as they moved down the street towards the wharves.

Stephan guided them straight to the first aid station, and without fuss and asking no questions the nurse set to work, stopping the nose bleed and checking for other injuries. She had obviously done this before.

While she was occupied, Rob checked Stephan's wallet. There was a considerable amount of money in it, so the beating was not robbery.

The nurse said, "I'll notify your boss. You're not

working tonight; go home and rest."

"Is there blood on my shirt? I don't want to worry my Ma."

"I've blotted out most of it, just get to bed."

The nurse called the car service used by the shipping company, and soon Rob and Stephan were home. Sarah was dozing over a book, so Rob quietly put Stephan to bed without disturbing her.

"Why did those men pick on you?" Rob asked quietly.

"They found my name in the company records," said Stephan. "I'm German, and I'm not going to discard my father's name for those thugs."

"I think you should consider a change of job," said Rob.

Stephan shook his head. "Not yet. A longshoreman makes good money. By spring, I should have enough to quit."

"Well, they didn't take your money, anyway," said Rob. He put the wallet on the bureau and added, "I'll see to it that your shirt is washed so your Ma won't know."

"Thank you, Rob. It was lucky you came by."

"It was, and I'm glad I did. Get some sleep."

As Rob climbed the stairs he thought maybe it was fate that I should help this particular young man?

23. A Party for the Season

A fortnight before Christmas, Sarah hosted a little party. She invited all her house guests; her neighbours with their children; the minister of the Lutheran Church, his wife and child; and the Rabbi and his wife and children. Rob and Dorie brought gifts for Sarah and Stephan, and were pleasantly surprised by a lovely Christmas tree standing in the parlour.

"My dear Hans loved Christmas. I want Stephan to have that tradition," said Sarah.

The tree hovered over a pile of gifts for everyone, especially the children. The doors to the dining room were thrown wide to reveal bowls of punch—a dark red one laced with sherry, and a light pink one for the children.

Dorie watched with pleasure as an animated and smiling Sarah instructed Stephan to pour the punch, and the children to open their presents which they did with gusto. Stephan suggested to Rob that they take the children to the back yard to play stick ball. Even the girls joined in that activity and the sun warmed the December day. When the sun ducked behind the tall, thick spruce, they all moved inside for sandwiches and lace cookies. Stephan played his accordion and they all sang carols. As the light began to fade, the guests faded too, with "Merry Christmas! Happy Hanukkah! and Good Wishes for a Peaceful New Year!" swirling through the air.

Rob and Dorie were loathe to leave before thanking Sarah for such a memorable party. As she bid goodnight to her guests, they sat on the chesterfield holding hands, enjoying the beautiful Christmas tree. Rob noticed a photograph on the mantle of two men holding a freshly cut fir tree. One held an axe. They were obviously related—perhaps brothers. And Rob knew for certain that the younger one was the one that he had killed in Kitcheners' Woods.

Sarah came in and seeing the object of Rob's gaze, said, "That is my Hans and his brother. Both are gone now. But I like that picture of them, and display it every Christmas." She smiled. "Would you like more punch?"

Rob and Dorie thanked her for the lovely party, and climbed the stairs to their home. Dorie chatted on about the party, not noticing Rob's silence. He was thinking, Stephan is my responsibility now; I hope I can take care of him.

A week later, Rob and Dorie sailed on the Britannia to Britannia Beach to spend Christmas with Dorie's parents.

24. Never White

Spring came early to usher in the roaring twenties, and with its purple crocuses and sunny forsythia came a special invitation and a visit from Betty, who arrived just as Dorie came home from classes.

Betty was sitting on the porch bench as Dorie came up the steps. Dorie was surprised and pleased, but her first thought was, What can I put together for a decent supper? How can I stretch our supper for three?

Betty hugged her, then held her at arm's length.

"Well, marriage certainly agrees with you, my dear. I'm happy I was part of your romantic wedding. Now, I won't have you fret about my unexpected visit. I know you've been in classes all day, so I've brought supper. But this news is so exciting, I had to share it with the matron of honour and the best man ... you look confused ... you haven't received the invitation yet. Open your mail and I will retrieve supper from the car."

Dorie let herself in, and picked up her mail on the hall table. She was not at all surprised, just relieved that Flo had set the date and considerately the wedding was set for after her own graduation. She and Rob had already been asked to be matron of honour and best man. Dorie smiled as she let in Betty and helped her up the stairs with the promised supper.

Betty chattered all the way up the stairs and into the tiny kitchen; she sat on a chair to catch her breath as Dorie opened the packages and distributed the contents into the oven and the icebox as required. Dorie poured two sherries and gestured to the parlour just as Betty caught up on her breathing and began to chatter again.

"My only niece, Flo, is almost a daughter to me, and with her mother all the way up in Britannia Beach, I'm sure they'll appreciate my assistance. A June wedding! Does the date agree with your commitments? Yes? Good! Flo has booked the church, so the next task is to plan the wedding dress. At least she won't be wearing green. She wears so much of that colour that she's in danger of turning into a frog!"

Betty was pacing the room, and gesturing in her animated fashion. Dorie relaxed, and sipped her sherry, thoroughly enjoying the performance.

"But—!" said Betty, with her left index finger pointing high in the air. She paused as she took a sip of her sherry, which she carried in her right hand. "But," she repeated, "it is clear that darling Flo cannot wear white!"

Dorie's eyebrow rose, wondering what Betty

insinuated.

Betty turned, and said, "She never could wear white, even as a toddler. I saw her once, dressed in white; her skin was whiter than her dress; I thought she was near death's door. I supplied all her pinafores after that, and I told my sister, never white!

"So!" Betty pivoted. "My sister is coming to town next week to choose fabric. I'm hoping we can find a cream satin and that you can come shopping so we can chose your fabric also … "

Dorie nodded. "Which day? Thursday is best for me."

"Thursday is perfect. It's settled. Is a shade of blue somewhat acceptable to you? Yes? Good. That will enhance Flo's colours. Next, I'll help the men. This is so exciting!"

Dorie finally managed to ask about Betty's household and that filled the time before Rob arrived home from work. When they finally said goodnight to Betty, after enjoying Tilly's creative supper, Rob and Dorie were exhausted, and went straight to bed.

With Betty at the helm Flo's wedding to Andy was smooth, lovely, and a little amusing because the bride and groom insisted that Beau and Digger be part of the wedding party. Their honeymoon at a cottage on Okanagan Lake also included the dogs.

By the end of June Dorie received notice that she had a teaching job in a brand new, two-room schoolhouse. As she told Rob the news, she said, "Now it's your turn, my love."

25. Reunion

After a beautifully sunny summer, Dorie began teaching, and Rob started taking classes at normal school. Stephan started university and a part-time job at Woodward's on Saturdays, thanks to Rob's recommendation. The department store offered Rob a part-time position too, rather than lose him, so the two rode the trolley together every Saturday.

Towards the end of the second week of school Rob said to Dorie, "I have a special friend that I would like to invite to dinner. Could you make your delicious pot roast for Saturday night?"

"Of course I can. I'll even make my lemon chiffon pie for dessert if you like? Who is your special friend?"

"Dorie, I can hardly believe it. His hair has turned white, and he's thinner, but it's Lewis, and he's teaching the history class at normal school."

"Definitely lemon chiffon pie!" said Dorie. "I'm looking forward to meeting Lewis at last. He was on my writing list you know, and he actually responded to my frivolous chatter."

The doorbell rang at exactly six o'clock on Saturday evening. Rob ran lightly down the stairs, but Sarah was already answering the door.

"Hello!" said Lewis. "I am expected for dinner by

Mr. and Mrs. Chase. My name is Lewis Hunter.

Rob arrived at that moment. "Lewis, may I present Sarah Smith, who owns this beautiful house, and happens to be our landlady."

"Indeed. I am charmed, Mrs. Smith," and Lewis kissed her hand.

Sarah lowered her eyes and Rob could swear she was flirting with Lewis.

"Ahem," said Rob. "As I mentioned, we are on the third floor," and he nodded towards the staircase.

"Of course, my friend. I am looking forward to meeting Dorie and enjoying a home-cooked meal."

The two crossed to the staircase, but Rob noted a lingering look pass between Lewis and Sarah. Well, I'll be! thought Rob to himself, and he sported a huge grin when he introduced Lewis to Dorie.

"I am delighted to meet you at last," said Dorie.

"And I, you, Dorie. The aroma of dinner tells me that it will far exceed your wonderful war cake!"

Dorie laughed, "and so it should. It's plain old pot roast, but it's Rob's favourite. I hope you enjoy it too."

"I'm certain that I shall, and a pot roast deserves a fine Merlot, which I brought for my charming hostess," said Lewis as he offered her a wrapped bottle.

As Dorie put the final touches on the dinner, Rob

and Lewis had an opportunity to catch up. Their voices were low, so Dorie missed most of it, but gave them some private time.

"After you left for Passchendale things stayed static," said Lewis. "No ground lost nor won. We dug a new trench at night; the old one was pretty putrid. A close bomb blast startled Axle and he ran away. Albert chased after and caught a bullet. Andy managed to get both of them back to the base hospital tent. Whatever happened to Andy?"

Rob filled him in on Andy and his new bride.

"Well, that's good," said Lewis. "Andy and Digger had an uncanny way of rescuing people. Anyway, we heard the Hindenburg line was broken, and took courage from that, and we were expecting an armistice soon. I suffered a piece of shrapnel in my leg, and Murray half-carried me back to the base camp hospital. The worst thing was the flu that hit the hospital at that time, and we all got sick. Sadly, Albert died. Sorry to tell you that after your saving his life in the woods. Anyway, I brought Axle home with me to Canada."

"Do you know what became of Murray?" asked Rob.

"Yes, I do," said Lewis. "Believe it or not, he stopped in Alberta and took work at a cattle ranch. Honestly, Rob, I feel sorry for his horse!"

As Rob and Lewis laughed at the thought of fat Murray on a swaybacked horse, Dorie called them to dinner.

Over the pot roast conversation revolved around teaching.

"Rob tells me you're teaching in the new two-room schoolhouse. How is that going?" asked Lewis.

"I love it," said Dorie. "The children are so bright and responsible without their mothers around. A classmate of mine from normal school and I are teaching the primary grades, from one to three. It's very satisfying."

"Good, I'm so glad someone as bright and caring as you are starting the little stinkers on the right path. It's such a waste of talent having wives stay home to embroider," said Lewis.

"Why weren't you teaching at the normal school while I was there?" asked Dorie.

"I was teaching high school while I finished the last term to obtain my degree," said Lewis. "Interrupted by the war, you understand.

"And you Rob," Lewis continued. "You still want to teach, I see."

Rob nodded. "Looking forward to it; I like kids"

"Yes, kids are cute enough when they're your own, but ..."

"But?" asked Rob.

"Quite frankly, my friend, you're too tall and too scary for the little ones. Not that you couldn't teach. I'm sure you'd be a great teacher, but I strongly advise that you concentrate on teaching high school students. You'd get their attention easily. You're good looking for the girls' attention, and you're tough enough to garner the boys' attention. Being a vet won't hurt either."

"That would take another year," said Rob.

"You know, Lewis is right, Rob," said Dorie. We can easily manage another year, so do it! Now how about dessert?"

Dorie served her lemon chiffon pie.

Lewis was impressed. "This pie could win a prize!"

Dorie and Rob laughed. "It already has!"

And the years passed happily as Rob finished school and began to teach high school. He replaced a retiring teacher, and the principal noticed that there was new interest in history on the part of the students.

26. I Take Thee for Granted

Rob and Dorie saw Andy and Flo on frequent weekends, and enjoyed watching Lewis's courtship of Sarah.

One Saturday, Dorie said, "Rob, I want to have a little talk with you."

"Fine," said Rob. "I'll be back later this afternoon. Stephan and I are running around Stanley Park. See you later, honey." With a kiss, he was off.

Rob returned later than expected. "Dorie, honey. Guess what?"

"I'm tired, Rob. I'm not in the mood for guessing."

"That's okay, hon. Stephan told me on our run that his classmate's parents are selling their house!"

"Good for them. Can I go to bed now?" said Dorie, with a yawn.

"No, not yet, Dorie," continued Rob. "That's why I'm so late. Stephan took me to their house to see it. The man came out of the house just as we got there. I expressed an interest and guess what? Oh, you don't want to guess. Tomorrow you and I are invited to view it—no agents—no for sale sign. We're going to see it at two in the afternoon. This is right for us, Dorie."

"We can't afford to buy a house now, Rob. I won't always be teaching, you know."

"Stephan says they don't want much. The house needs some fixing, so it's perfect."

"Calm down, Rob. You haven't even seen it all yet."

"I know, but it looks great from the outside, and the yard is spacious. I have a hunch this is it, Dorie."

"Well then, I guess we'd better look at your 'hunch,'" said Dorie, and with a kiss she went to bed.

And so they viewed the house. Dorie loved it too, and the elderly couple were relieved that they liked Rob and Dorie. They felt their home would be loved and cared for.

Rob caught a jitney to take them home. He thought Dorie looked a little tired.

In the car, Dorie said, "I have something to tell you, Rob."

"Good, honey. I have something to tell you, too. It's good news. I've made a small investment on Betty's advice, and it has made enough to pay a healthy down payment and keep our mortgage payments really low. So you won't have to work if you don't want to."

Dorie said, "About that, Rob. I have something to say."

"Whatever you decide, sweetheart," said Rob. "Here we are, home for now."

There followed bank meetings, mortgage arrangements, movers booked, and packing and shopping for the new house. Time flew in the midst of such responsibilities.

Moving day arrived. Rob asked Sarah to look after Dorie. "She's looking a little peaked. Teaching is tiring, you know. Stephan and I can handle the move, and Betty's coming to help too."

Dorie protested, but Rob insisted, so she spent a quiet day dozing on Sarah's couch. And Sarah, with a gleam in her eye, made her snacks all day long.

Finally, Betty came to take Dorie to her new home. Dorie and Sarah made their tearful goodbyes, and shortly after Betty drove into the driveway of the new house. She cut the engine and said, "Dorie, everything is unpacked. Tilly and Max were a wonderful help as usual, and Tilly's made a light supper for you and Rob."

"Thank you, Betty. How can I ever repay you?" asked Dorie.

Betty laughed. "By telling Rob!"

"It's not easy … " mumbled Dorie.

"I know," said Betty, her mouth twisted in humour. "He's pretty obsessed at the moment. But …. tell him before someone else does."

Dorie walked into the house. Rob took her on a

tour of her new home. It was in remarkable order, but Rob had placed his desk in the wrong bedroom to start his den, and Dorie was upset.

Rob was puzzled. "Well, let's move it then. You take that side. It's not loaded yet, so it's light."

Dorie burst out crying, "Move it yourself!" and went to bed without supper.

The next day, Andy and Flo arrived to see the new house. While they toured the house, Flo oddly kept her big purse on her shoulder. At last they sat in the living room for tea and cookies, and leftovers from Tilly's supper.

"Actually, we have a housewarming present for you," Flo announced.

Dorie smiled. "That's thoughtful, Flo. I wondered about the big package you left in the front hall."

Flo said quickly, "Oh, that's not it. It's here in my purse."

She reached into her purse, and brought out a ball of black fur.

"It's Digger's puppy! We thought it was about time, especially with your new house. He's almost trained, and his food and bedding are in the front hall. He responds to growls and woofs from Digger and Beau, but we find he responds to 'Bertie' too. You can call him whatever you wish. I hope you're pleased … but …" Flo looked at Dorie cuddling the puppy. "I see that you are."

Rob was grinning from ear to ear.

As they left, Flo hugged Dorie tightly. "Are you okay? Is the pup too much? Does Rob know?"

Dorie gave a little laugh. "Not yet, but tonight, he's going to listen if I have to tie him to a chair!"

After Flo and Andy left, Rob said, "I'm going to move those boxes to the basement corner, so I can plan for a shop."

"No, Rob. I have something to tell you."

"I'll only be a few minutes, Dorie," said Rob.

"And I've only waited for weeks. This can't wait, Rob! Sit in that chair, or I'll tie you to it! I mean it!"

Astonished, Rob sat meekly in the chair.

Dorie began, "I'm ..." The puppy came over to her, and leapt into her lap. She laid her hand on the soft fur, and started again. "I'm going to have a human baby to play with our new puppy."

The word 'baby' took several seconds to absorb into Rob's brain. Then his eyes grew so big they were almost all white. He rose to his feet, put the puppy aside, and took Dorie into his arms.

"We are the luckiest people in the world," he said.

"I know," she whispered.

Marian Keen

About Marian Keen

A seasoned children's and young adult Canadian author, Marian Keen has written her first adult novel, Jewel of Britannia, set in British Columbia, Canada, during WWI. A strong dedication to historical accuracy and vibrant storytelling contribute to her success. Marian lives in Metro Vancouver with her husband.

Other works by Marian Keen include:

Verity
Lexi and Hippocrates Find Trouble at the Olympics
Lexi and Imhotep to the Rescue
Lexi and Lister Defeat Death
Lexi and Marie Curie Saving Lives in World War I
Alex and the Spirit of Christmas
Abigail Skunk's Lessons for her Kits

Keen Ideas Publishing
Vancouver, Canada

www.keenideaspublishing.com